Deception in Denmark

Dan DeKoning

ISBN: 978-1-963691-00-9

DEDICATION

This book is dedicated to all you geocachers out there who keep the game interesting. From the hiders, to the finders, to those who host events, and those who keep things running at HQ. Thank you all for giving me a reason to get outside in the sunshine… and the rain… and the snow…

Deception in Denmark

CHAPTER ONE

"It's beautiful here," Allie Ashe said as she looked over the Baltic Sea. She watched as two ferries passed each other out in the strait and a plane descending into Copenhagen Kastrup Airport. She didn't recognize the colors on the aircraft, so she figured the plane was one of the many European carriers coming in for a landing.

"I told you that you guys would love it here," Ingrid Snyder said. "I'm so excited to show you around my home country."

Ingrid took off her hat, exposing her shoulder-length blond hair that looked almost white in the summer sun. She adjusted her ponytail and stuck the hat back on her head. She looked at Allie with her ice-blue eyes and smiled.

"Hey, are you two going to help us out here, or what?" Geneva Benson said. She'd been hard at work trying to find a geocache, presumably hidden in a retaining wall. "Drake is just about clueless over here."

"Okay, so I resemble that remark," Drake Decker said as he yanked a wad of seaweed from the wall, chucked it on the ground, and investigated the hole he pulled it from. "I can't help it. I abhor wall caches."

"Did you check the cache description for any hints?" Allie asked as she wandered over to Geneva's side.

"I don't remember. I read the description pretty quickly, and I can't recall if I even noticed if there was a hint or not," Geneva said.

Allie took her phone from the rear pocket of her pants. She checked the geocaching app, pulled up the cache they were looking for, and carefully read the description and checked all aspects of the geocache page. "You're right. There are no hints. According to some logs, though, it seems the coordinates are off between ten and twenty feet, depending on who found the thing."

"Ten or twenty feet?" Drake asked. "That's all? No direction and no corrected coordinates? No hint or pictures of the hiding spot?"

Allie stuck her nose back in her phone and read through everything again. "Nope," she said. "That's all I can tell you based on the logs. At least, the ones in English that I can read." She checked the app and went to where the coordinates said ground zero was. Near her feet, she found a stick, so she picked it up and jabbed it into the sand, so the stick stood straight toward the sky.

Allie looked up and spotted Geneva staring at her.

"What?" Allie asked.

"Where did you get those pants?" Geneva asked.

Allie looked down at what she was wearing. The pants she'd put on that morning were mustard yellow in color, and printed on them were several types of mushrooms, snails, flowers, and ladybugs in various shades of red, brown, white, and green. "Are you teasing me?"

"No, actually," Geneva said. "I really like them. I've never seen anything like them before."

Allie studied Geneva's face, and to her surprise, Geneva

looked serious. "Oh, well, thank you. If you want, I'll tell you where I got them and you can get a pair of your own."

"Super!" Geneva said.

"Hey," Drake said, "are you two going to help us out here, or what?"

"I did help," Allie said. "This stick marks ground zero. We need to check twenty feet on either side, and we should find it somewhere within that radius."

Allie started looking in the wall directly to the left of the stick, and since Geneva was only a foot from her, she moved a few feet from Allie and started her investigation as well. Drake and Ingrid got the hint and started their search to the right of the stick.

The two pairs put their full attention on the wall, all four friends hoping to find the geocache first. Ten minutes elapsed and Geneva and Ingrid simultaneously pulled containers from the wall and held them in the air.

"Got it!" the friends exclaimed in unison.

Allie raised an eyebrow. A sparkle of sunlight reflected off her green eyes as she stepped closer to Geneva. "Two containers? Is one a dummy or a throw-down?"

Geneva turned the tin box in her hands, looking for a latch, but she discovered no way to open it. It was four inches square and two inches thick. Crude soldering sealed the seams, and when Geneva shook the box, both she and Allie heard something rattle inside.

"What do you suppose that is?" Allie asked.

"I don't know," Geneva said as she brushed sand from the box.

"Hey, are you guys coming over?" Ingrid yelled from thirty feet away.

"Should I put this back?" Geneva asked.

"Where did you find it?" Allie asked.

Geneva bent over and pointed to a gap in the wall, less than a foot above the ground. "In there."

Allie had to get on one knee and bend over to peer into the gap. "How in the world did you even spot that?"

"Just luck. It caught a glint of sunlight. At first, I thought it was only a gum wrapper or a piece of aluminum foil."

Allie got back to her feet and brushed the sand from her pants. "I'd say keep it. It'll be fun to see what's in it. Maybe it's some secret Danish treasure."

Geneva shook the box again. Inside, something moved. "Whatever it is, it can't be much."

Allie shrugged. "Okay, so it's the missing ring of an old royal family. Come on. They're waiting for us."

Allie and Geneva followed the wall for thirty feet and caught up to Ingrid and Drake. Ingrid passed Allie a long strip of paper, and Allie reached for the pen that was wedged into her baseball cap over her right ear. She added her geocaching nickname to the paper, then passed both items to Geneva, who jotted down her credentials. When she finished, Geneva handed the pen to Allie and the paper to Ingrid.

Ingrid folded the log and tucked it into a plastic bag she held. Once she closed it, Drake handed her a four-inch-long black plastic tube. She placed the log in the tube, snapped the lid shut, slid the tube into the wall, and placed a rock in front of it.

"There," Ingrid said. "You got your first find in Denmark. Congratulations to all of you."

"Great," Drake said. "Could we go take a nap now?"

Ingrid checked her phone. "Sorry, Drake. We can't check into the hotel for another three hours. I promise after a few more geocaches, you'll get your second wind and forget all about that nap."

Drake rolled his eyes. "Fine. Can we at least find a snack?"

Ingrid grinned. "That we can do, my friend."

Twenty minutes later, Ingrid handed Drake a plate.

"What is this?" Drake asked.

"Just try it."

Drake picked up the open-faced sandwich and smelled it. Although he scrunched his nose, to his credit, he took a bite of the corner. He chewed for a moment, nodded, and swallowed. "That's not bad. What is it?"

"It's Leverpostej," Ingrid said. "A liver pâté covered with bacon and sautéed mushrooms."

Drake popped the last of the sandwich in his mouth and swallowed it down. "I like this, and you're right, I got my second wind. Where to now?"

"Want to see a mermaid?" Ingrid asked. "There are a few geocaches over that way."

Thirty minutes later Ingrid scored a parking space a stone's throw from St. Alban's church, and everyone got out and checked out the Neo-Gothic structure and its tall, pointed spire.

"Is there a cache here?" Geneva asked.

Ingrid checked her app. "No, but it looks like there's one over by the fountain, about a hundred feet from here."

Ingrid double-checked her phone and walked toward the sculpture.

"This is amazing, too," Geneva said as they moved closer. "What is this of?"

"It depicts the Norse goddess Gefion, who plowed the land with her four sons, that she transformed into oxen," Drake said.

"How in the world did you know that?" Geneva asked, impressed by Drake's knowledge.

Drake grinned and took a step to his left. When he did, everyone else saw the information sign he'd been standing directly in front of.

Geneva laughed and playfully rolled her eyes. "My hero."

"According to the hint, they hid the geocache at the rear of the statue," Ingrid said. The large fountain had a waist-high concrete wall around it, and on the fountain side of the wall was a ring of large rocks. Ingrid moved to the point on the wall where she was directly behind the statue. She leaned over the top of the wall and spotted a bit of orange underneath a rock the size of a large potato. She moved the rock and retrieved a plastic matchstick holder from the fountain.

"Got it," Ingrid said as she got back to her feet. She unscrewed the cover and removed the paper log from the container. She took Allie's pen, signed her name, and passed the log to the others. Once everyone signed, Ingrid stowed the geocache back under the rock and led the group away from the fountain and along the grass-lined path of the promenade.

From where they started, they'd walked over a tenth of a mile when Ingrid checked her phone and pointed to a four-person picnic table ahead.

"There's a cache over there," Ingrid said as she led the group off-trail and onto the grass. She took a seat on the picnic table, Drake took the seat next to her, and Geneva and Allie remained standing.

Geneva checked her geocaching app, discovered they were standing just about on top of one of them, checked the description, and offered her phone to Ingrid. "Can you translate this for me?"

Ingrid glanced at Geneva's phone and waved it away. "I'm looking at the same cache. Other is the container size, and the description just gives a generic overview of the area."

"Any hint?" Drake asked.

"Nope," Ingrid said. "The logs aren't much help either, except to say that the coordinates are pretty much dead on. That tells me it's either on that bench or in this tree. Anyone have a search preference?"

"I'll take the table," Drake said. He demonstrated his eagerness to search for the geocache by taking off his hat and placing it on the table. He ran his fingers through his hair a few times and shrugged out of his backpack to retrieve a bottle of water.

Ingrid set her phone on the table and leaned over until she was lying on the bench. From there, she began searching the underside of the table.

"I guess we know what their preferences are," Allie said to Geneva. "Shall we check out this tree?"

"We shall," Geneva agreed.

Allie and Geneva moved to the beech tree growing a few feet away from the picnic table. Allie could tell the tree was a fairly new one since it stood only seven feet tall and the trunk was only a foot in diameter. When she stood on her tiptoes, she could run her hand on the fork where the trunk divided into two. She felt something, grasped it, and pulled it down.

"What did you find?" Geneva asked.

Allie opened her hand. "Leaves. Did you find anything in the trunk?"

"There's nothing to find. There are no holes in it, no spaces, not even a rock to hide things under."

Allie dropped the leaves and instinctively moved to rub her hands on her pants. She stopped herself just in time and brushed them on the grass instead. She turned her attention to the picnic table where Ingrid had moved one seat to the right, and Drake was down on his knees, investigating under his seat.

"Got it!" Ingrid said, as she pulled something out from under the table. She held aloft a pocket cache, which was a small three-by-two-inch plastic bag covered in white duct tape to match the color of the table. Inside was a magnet, which held it tight against the metal frame.

"Good find," Geneva said.

Ingrid sat, opened the cache, and signed the log, and passed it around to the others. Once everyone signed, she placed it back where she found it.

"Where's the mermaid?" Allie asked.

Ingrid pointed down at the promenade. "That way. We only need to follow the path. Once we come across a large crowd, then we'll know we've arrived."

The group followed the trail, and as Ingrid had said, the closer they got to the iconic statue, the more the tourist traffic increased. After two-tenths of a mile, they stopped, and Ingrid, Allie, and Geneva took a seat on a park bench behind a mass of people.

"What are we waiting for?" Drake asked, rocking impatiently on his feet. "Let's go see it."

"Be patient," Ingrid said. "Give it like ten minutes and all those people will climb back on the tour buses behind us, and we'll have the entire place almost to ourselves."

Drake moved behind the bench and did his best to stand still while he watched the hundred people jockey for positions to take photographs. From behind him, he heard a whistle, and he turned in time to see the tour guide from the lead bus standing on the bus steps and waving a red and white flag attached to a retractable stick. When he faced forward again, he realized he had just seen the sign for people to return to the buses, which the crowd did.

The four friends waited as the strangers passed them, headed for their ride, and once the coast was clear, Ingrid stood and led her companions to a metal railing at the edge of the sidewalk. In the harbor a few feet from them sat *The Little Mermaid,* a bronze beauty leisurely perched on a rock as if waiting for her prince to come along.

"She's pretty," Allie said. "I like that green patina."

Allie removed her phone from her pocket and took several photographs.

"There's a virtual cache here," Ingrid said.

"Is it a hard one?" Drake asked.

Ingrid read the cache description. "Not really. We need to answer a couple of questions and take a photo with the statue in the background. If you don't want to show your face, you can snap a picture of your hand pointing at it."

Geneva handed her phone to Allie and grabbed Drake by the arm. "Come on, fella, come and take a picture with me."

Allie held up Geneva's phone and made sure they were within the frame, then issued directions. "Separate your heads a few inches. I can't get the statue in there. Okay, good. Now, Drake, turn your head like you're going to kiss Geneva on the cheek. That's it. Lower your head. Okay. Hold those poses right there."

Rather than take just one picture, Allie fired off a half dozen of them in quick sequence, then handed the phone back.

Geneva looked at the pictures and laughed, the specks of gold and green in her hazel eyes catching the afternoon sunlight.

"What's so funny?" Drake asked.

Rather than answer, Geneva turned her phone so he could see the picture, which Allie had framed, so it looked like Drake was kissing the statue.

"It looks like you have a new girlfriend," Geneva joked and laughed again.

"Ha. Ha. Not funny," Drake said, crossing his arms and taking a step back to show his displeasure.

Geneva moved toward him and planted a kiss on his cheek. "It's okay. I still love you, even though you've found another woman."

"Come on, take our picture," Ingrid said.

Geneva spun around and took Ingrid's phone. Ingrid and Allie took a position on one side of the statue, and Geneva got the shot. She handed the phone back, and Ingrid checked the photo.

"What are the questions?" Geneva asked.

Ingrid checked. "How many diagonal rocks are beneath where she's sitting, and what is she holding in her hand?"

Allie, Drake, and Geneva returned to the fence and looked carefully at the statue.

"I'd say one diagonal rock," Drake said. "I'm not sure what that is in her lap. A shirt? A fishing net?"

"It looks like a shirt to me," Allie said. "Why don't you go out there and see for sure?"

"No, but thanks."

"Okay," Ingrid said. "Shirt it is. Someone take some close-up photos of her, and I'll submit my answers. If it turns out they're wrong, we can look at the photos for the right one."

Ingrid's phone rang. She answered, had a quick conversation in Danish, then returned to logging her cache. Once she'd finished, she turned her attention back to her friends. "That was the hotel. Our rooms are ready. Who's ready for a change of clothes or a nap?"

Allie, Drake, and Geneva all raised their hands at once.

"Come on, then. Back the way we came," Ingrid said, taking Allie by the hand.

The group strolled back to the rental car, and everyone piled in. Ingrid drove away, then four minutes later cursed in Danish when she turned down a one-way road headed in the opposite direction from where she wanted to go.

"Everything okay?" Allie asked.

Ingrid nodded. "We'll be fine just as soon as I get us going the right way."

"Hey!" Drake yelled from the back seat. "Pull in here!"

Startled, Ingrid smashed the brakes, causing all her passengers to lurch forward and strain their seatbelts. She pulled into a parking space and stopped.

"What's the matter?" Ingrid asked as she spied Drake in the rearview mirror.

"Nothing. Sorry about that. Geneva, do you still have that box you found?"

Geneva nodded. Her backpack was at her feet, and she rummaged through it until she found the tiny tin box. She handed it to Drake and was about to ask a question, but Drake opened the door.

"Everyone wait here. I'll be right back," he ordered.

The women watched as he took the small box and jogged in the direction from which they'd come.

"What do you suppose that was all about?" Geneva asked.

Allie sighed. "Well, although we've been friends forever, when it comes to Drake, sometimes I still don't know what he's thinking."

CHAPTER TWO

The next morning, Allie was in the middle of a cup of tea when Geneva and Drake entered the breakfast area of the hotel.

"Good morning," Allie said. "Sleep well?"

Geneva cocked a thumb at Drake. "He was fast asleep before I even got out of the shower."

Drake smiled and shrugged. "Y'all understand I'm not good with time zone changes. Give me a week or two, and I'll catch up to the rest of you."

Allie drained the remains of her tea and set the mug on the table. "By the time you catch up, we'll on our way home."

Drake raised an eyebrow, then looked toward the breakfast buffet. "Did y'all eat?"

"Not yet. I'm waiting for Ingrid," Allie said.

"Where is she?" Geneva asked.

"When I left her, she was still in the shower. Like Drake here, she had a little trouble getting up this morning."

Drake grinned. "See, I'm not the only one who has trouble with long-distance flights."

"It wasn't the flight. She stayed up almost all night talking to people on the phone."

"To whom?" Geneva asked.

Allie shrugged. "Couldn't tell you. It was all in Danish."

"You're learning Danish," Drake pointed out. "You couldn't eavesdrop on anything?"

"Only when she said hi or bye. That was about it." Allie stood and picked up her mug. "I'm going to get more tea while I wait."

"Wait for what?" Ingrid asked as she entered the room, her hair still wet.

"For you, as always," Allie said. She smiled, gave Ingrid a hug, and swatted her on the butt. "Come on. Let's eat. I'm starving."

Not having to be told twice, Drake led the way to the buffet line, picked up a plate, then stared at the options. Before him there were a variety of breads, cold cuts, cheeses, jam, fresh fruit, yogurt, cereal, porridge, eggs, sausages, and a delicious selection of pastries.

While Drake tried to determine what he wanted, Ingrid selected some yogurt and two pastries, while Geneva and Allie went with the scrambled eggs with a side of sausages and toast with fresh jam. Drake made himself a breakfast sandwich composed of scrambled eggs and sliced ham.

Allie and Geneva dropped their plates off at the table, then returned to retrieve beverages for everyone. Allie refreshed her tea and got a mug for Ingrid, while Geneva poured glasses of orange juice for herself and Drake. When they returned, they found Ingrid picking at a pastry while Drake was already halfway through his sandwich.

"Good?" Geneva asked.

"Mm-hmm," Drake said as he chewed.

"What adventures do you have planned out for us today, Ingrid?" Geneva asked in between forkfuls of eggs.

Ingrid put the pastry on her plate and wiped her hands. "I

have a few options I will present to you. First, though, I'm dying to learn what's in the bag?"

"What bag?" Geneva asked.

"Yesterday, when Drake had me pull over, he jumped out of the car and returned with a bag. Surely you didn't forget that bit of odd behavior."

"I didn't, actually. I was going to come by last night, but sleepyhead had other plans." Geneva leaned down and retrieved a nondescript black plastic bag from her backpack. She placed it on the table in the center, then finished the last of her eggs and moved the plate aside.

From the bag, she removed the tin box she'd found and dropped the bag to the ground.

"It's the box. Drake got it open for me."

"How did he do that?" Allie asked.

"Spotted a metal shop. I walked in and asked if they would get it open," Drake said as he wiped his fingertips on a napkin. "The guy took one glance at me, took the box, and came back three minutes later. Not only was the box open, but he gave us that nice keepsake bag to put it in."

"Okay. But what's in the box?" Ingrid asked.

Geneva carefully lifted the lid and placed it on the side. From inside, she withdrew a coin, a torn photograph, and a small scrap of blue paper with a set of coordinates on it, along with a few words of Danish.

"Can you read that?" Geneva asked Ingrid.

"May I touch this stuff?" Ingrid asked.

"Go ahead," Geneva said.

Ingrid turned the paper around so she could see it better. The writing was in cursive, and part of it had faded, but she still made it out. "It says 'for the brave'."

Ingrid picked up the photograph. Although the bottom half was missing, she noticed it was a soldier. "I think this is from World War II," she said. She placed the picture on the table and picked up the coin. She took a quick glance at it, then brought it closer to her eye and studied it intently. "This is much older. I think this is a Viking coin."

"As in Minnesota?" Drake asked.

Ingrid shook her head. "As in the people who really discovered America."

"What do you suppose these things are?" Allie asked.

"I don't know," Ingrid said. "But I know someone who might."

Ingrid removed her phone from her back pocket and made a phone call. When the person on the other end answered, Ingrid spoke in Danish and in hushed tones for five minutes, then hung up.

"Well, I figured out what we're doing today. First thing on the agenda is to go see my friend, Asger, over at the museum. He says he can meet us at his office at four this afternoon. That gives us a whole day to kill. Who's up to finding a few geocaches?"

* * *

Asger Berg's fingers trembled as he studied the photograph. At first glance, it looked like nothing more than a photo of a German soldier with a stoic expression somewhere in Scandinavia using a glacier as a spectacular backdrop. He'd expected a photo from eighty years ago to be faded, but other than it being torn in half, it looked like it got developed only a few days ago. As a curator in the Danish Resistance Museum, Asger had seen hundreds of photos similar to this one. Except for the nearly imperceptible series of marks along the top edge of the photograph. Most people would have dismissed it as damage to the nearly century-old print, but Asger's trained eye recognized it as a deliberate pattern.

"Might it be...?" Asger murmured.

"Might it be what?" Ingrid asked, leaning over Asger's desk

to get a better look.

Asger enjoyed one of the smallest offices in the museum and could only fit two others in the crowded space with him. Ingrid and Geneva occupied his guest chairs while Drake and Allie explored the museum.

"Hold on. Give me a minute," Asger said. He rummaged through the top drawer of his desk and extracted a magnifying glass. With that, he took a closer look at the marks. "Where did you say you found this?"

"In a geocache," Geneva said.

"It was part of the retaining wall near where we used to fish as kids," Ingrid added.

Asger spun the photo around and handed Ingrid the glass. "Look on the upper edge."

Ingrid took the magnifying glass and held it to the picture. It took her a moment, then she caught it. "Is that a code?"

Asger nodded. "I think it's a substitution cipher. It looks like a simple one, but it's still in code."

"Are you sure?" Ingrid asked.

"Yes. Between my time at the university and working in this museum, I've seen plenty of these. Usually, members of the Danish Resistance used them when the Nazis occupied the country."

"Do you think you can break it?" Geneva asked.

Asger didn't respond and instead reached for a pad of paper. He copied the code from the photo to the paper, then went to work trying to solve the cipher. After several false starts, recognizable words began to form. When he finished, he put his pen on the desk and picked up the notepad.

"Treasures hidden. Ryvangen. Beneath the fallen," he said. His voice rose in pitch, and his eyes glowed with excitement.

Asger leaned back in his chair, took off his glasses, and rubbed his eyes.

"Does that mean anything to you?" Ingrid asked.

"Ryvangen, sure. It's a site of a memorial park on the north side of town. It commemorates members of the Danish Resistance who the Germans executed during World War II. The words 'beneath the fallen' have no meaning to me, though. If they put cipher on this photograph around the same time they took it, it could mean just about anything. Ryvangen as a park has been around forever, but of course the memorial didn't come to be until years after the war ended. Or it might be that the cipher got added to the photo years after it happened. There's no way to tell, really."

"What about this?" Geneva asked, picking up the coin. "Can you tell us anything about it?"

Asger took the coin from her and used his magnifying glass on it. "Looks authentic. It's a Viking coin. Several hundred years old."

"Is it worth anything?" Geneva asked.

Asger placed it on the table next to the photograph. "Not as much as you would think, considering how old it is. At best, you could get a few hundred American dollars for it."

Asger reached forward and put the coin in Geneva's palm. "Keep it. It's a nice little souvenir." He checked the clock on the wall and noticed it was nearly closing time. "If you'll excuse me, I need to see you out. I have some phone calls to return before I leave for the day."

Ingrid and Geneva stood at the same time.

"Of course," Ingrid said. "Thank you for your time."

She leaned forward and kissed her old friend on both cheeks.

"Will you be in town long?" Asger asked.

"A few days," Ingrid said.

Asger moved from behind his desk and ushered the women outside his door. "Ring me, and we'll get a coffee, okay?"

"That sounds good to me," Ingrid said.

"And please, bring your charming friend," Asger said as he closed the door.

Since Asger summarily dismissed them, the women started walking down the corridor that led from the museum offices to the main exhibit space.

"Nice guy," Geneva said. "How long have you known him?"

"Practically my entire life," Ingrid said. "As a boy, he lived across the lane from my aunt and uncle."

"How much do you trust him?"

Ingrid stopped in her tracks and turned to face Geneva. "I haven't seen him in years. We've only kept in touch via email. What makes you ask that question?"

"I don't understand it. I got the idea that he wasn't being completely honest with us. And I noticed you didn't show him the paper with the coordinates on it."

Ingrid gave Geneva a small smile. "Those I thought we could figure out on our own."

* * *

Allie checked for traffic before she crossed the street, glad that she did since there was a group of bike riders racing up the road. As she waited for them to pass, she checked her phone. She was already fifteen minutes later than she intended to be, but since she had no texts from any of her traveling companions, she figured Ingrid was still talking to local friends, and Geneva and Drake were still in the process of rising and shining.

She got a surprise, though, when she was walking past the breakfast room, she spotted her three friends enjoying their morning meal. Drake must have said something funny, because Geneva and Ingrid were laughing so hard that Geneva began coughing violently enough that Ingrid needed to slap her on the back.

"Hey guys," Allie said when she approached the table.

Everyone stopped laughing and looked at her, struggling to hold their composure.

"What?" Allie asked.

No one said a word.

"Come on," Allie persuaded. "What's so funny?"

Geneva took a deep breath and looked Allie square in the eyes. "Did you once get attacked by a butterfly?"

Allie scrunched her face while she searched for the memory.

"That time we were in Texas? Down near San Antonio?" Drake hinted. "We'd just found that cache with that black widow spider the size of a quarter nearby?"

Allie smiled as the memory came back. "Oh. That was nothing. A butterfly landed on my neck as we were walking back to the car. Not a big deal."

"Not a big deal?" Drake said. "That's not the way I remember it." Drake stood. "She was walking a few steps in front of me, and this butterfly landed on the side of her neck. Allie panicked, screamed 'spider', then started slapping at her neck while simultaneously spinning in circles." As he told the story, Drake demonstrated the actions. "She did that for a good five minutes before she realized it was nothing."

Allie crossed her arms and rolled her eyes. "Hey, it was a traumatic event for me."

Drake took Allie into a hug. "I'm sorry. I remember it was."

"Wait," Ingrid interrupted. "What happened to the butterfly?"

"Well…"

Two hours later, the group arrived at Ryvangen Memorial Park. Although they realized they were there for a specific purpose, they split into groups and wandered around the historical site that commemorated the Danish resistance fighters during World War II. Included in the grounds were over one hundred graves of resistance fighters, a memorial stone dedicated to ninety-one resistance members, and a memorial wall with plaques honoring those whose remains they couldn't find.

South of the memorial part of the park was a large public green space that contained hundreds of trees, walking and bike paths, and facilities for tennis and soccer.

"This is a big place," Allie said as she reached Ingrid, who was reading the inscription on a memorial.

Ingrid turned around and looked at the expanse of land. "Too big. Beneath the fallen isn't a whole lot to go on. There are too many places to check."

Allie nodded. "Literally hundreds of them."

"Where should we start looking?"

Allie shrugged. "Right here, I guess."

Allie and Ingrid began to circle the monument, their eyes scanning it and the ground, looking for anything unusual. Being geocachers, they both had a knack for noticing things that were out of the ordinary, since many geocaches were often hidden right in plain sight.

Both women were so focused on the search that they almost collided with an elderly man who had approached silently.

"I'm so sorry," Allie said as she stopped just before making contact with him. "I didn't see you there."

The old man waved off the apology. "No harm done," he said in English with a heavy Danish accent. "Are you from America?"

Allie nodded.

"Well, welcome to Denmark. You must have some Danish in you," the man said, noticing Ingrid.

"Yes," Ingrid said. "Both of my parents are from here, although they live in the states now."

The man pointed at the monument. "It's good to see someone taking such an interest in our history. Who did you say your parents are? Perhaps I know them. I've lived around Copenhagen my entire life."

"They're name is Snyder, although you probably wouldn't know them. They're from Aalborg."

"Snyder? That's not a Danish name."

"I know. My great-grandparents were Dutch, and they brought the name with them when they moved to Denmark a century ago."

"My name is Jens Dalgaard," the old man replied, extending his hand.

Allie and Ingrid both shook his hand.

"I was just a boy during the occupation, but I remember it well," Jens said, gesturing toward the monument. "My uncle was one of the ones executed here."

Ingrid noticed as Allie arched an eyebrow, then turned her attention back to the man. "Mr. Dalgaard, I wonder if I might ask you something. Have you ever heard any stories about… well, about things being hidden here in this park? During the war, I mean."

The old man's eyes narrowed slightly. "Hidden things? Like treasure? Now that's an interesting question." He stopped speaking and was silent for a long moment. "You know, there were always rumors. Whispers of resistance fighters burying weapons, documents… even valuables either taken from the Germans or squirreled away so they wouldn't fall into German hands. But, other than a few pocket watches and an occasional knife or a handful of coins, no one ever found anything, so far as I know."

"Did any of the rumors mention a specific location?" Allie asked. "Perhaps near this monument?"

Jens gave her a long look. "You two are up to something, aren't you? Something that's led you here."

Allie hesitated, then nodded once to confirm the man's suspicions. "Possibly, but we're not sure what it means."

Jens sighed. "Be careful, girls. The past has a way of reaching into the present, and not always for the better. If there are secrets buried here, perhaps they're best left that way."

Without another word beyond his cryptic warning, Jens

Dalgaard turned and slowly walked away, leaving Allie and Ingrid standing by the monument.

"Who was that?" Geneva asked as she approached Allie and Ingrid, with Drake right behind her.

"A local," Ingrid said, relaying everything to them that Jens had said.

"It doesn't seem right that the coordinates would tell us they buried something here beneath the fallen," Geneva said. "From a sign we read, they didn't erect these monuments until long after the war was over. Maybe that code was nothing more than a prank. Or maybe a red herring planted by the Germans to mislead the resistance somehow."

"That could be, but Asger seemed to think it was authentic," Ingrid said.

Geneva scrunched her face, then nodded to agree. "He did. If he thought there was something to it, then why would the clue bring us to a place that didn't exist until years after that photo got taken?"

"But it did exist," Drake said, getting in on the conversation. "Even though these memorials weren't here during the war, something must have been. It's not like this was empty space. It could be there was a building or whatever here during that time that isn't here now."

"You think we'll be able to find a hidden treasure based on a building that hasn't stood here for eighty years?" Geneva asked. "How do you expect us to do that?"

Drake pointed at her pants. "Why don't we try using those coordinates you have in your pocket?"

CHAPTER THREE

Geneva reached into her pocket, pulled out a small plastic bag, and held it up for her friends to see.

"Great. Where do those lead to?" Drake asked.

Geneva took a moment and entered them into her app, checked the position, and pointed toward the east. "Four hundred and twelve feet that way."

With Geneva taking the lead, the group wandered toward the far boundary of the memorial park. They transitioned from a well-maintained lawn to taller grass, then slipped into a copse of trees.

"It's not much farther. Under ninety feet now," Geneva said, referencing her phone.

As the trees closed in, the group had to switch from walking in pairs to single file. After fifteen yards of tight quarters, the path widened, and the group found themselves standing beside a stone wall, mostly concealed by tall grass, fallen tree limbs, and untold decades of other debris. The wall, looking like it had stood for at least a hundred years, appeared constructed of large river rocks in various shapes, sizes, and colors, held in position by what seemed to be a rudimentary mud and straw mortar.

"This looks more like something might be beneath or inside," Drake said. "Please tell me we're right on top of the coordinates."

Geneva checked the number and shook her head. "Sorry. Best I can give you is ten feet."

Drake shrugged. "We've found things with more of a variance."

"We have," Allie agreed. "But those were geocaches we were looking for, so we knew we had a chance of finding something going in. This could be a wild goose chase, and we might need pruning shears and a hoe to find this thing, if not excavation equipment."

"Do you think we need to be on the other side of that wall?" Ingrid asked.

Allie stepped back and examined the situation more closely. Where they stood, she estimated parts of the wall were at least six feet tall. Although she couldn't tell where it began or ended, based on the general shape of the vegetation in the area, she assumed it was eight to ten feet in length.

"I don't know," Allie said, answering Ingrid's question. "I wish there was a way to at least see on the other side of it."

"Come on over here and I'll give you a boost," Drake said.

He put his back to the wall and crouched, interlocking his fingers. Without an invitation, Allie put her right foot into his hands and bounced on her right leg. Since it was a maneuver the geocaching friends had performed on multiple occasions, they completed the act without saying a word between them. When Allie was at the apex of her bounce, Drake lifted her in the air. Allie reached for the top of the wall, and when she did, she pulled the top rock, one the approximate size of a basketball, and it shifted toward her.

"Put me down!" Allie screamed, letting go of the rock.

Drake bent over and let go of Allie's foot. The second she hit the ground, she pushed Drake to the side and moved away from the wall. The stone landed with a muted thunk right where Drake had been. Together, the four of them stood staring at the stone for a moment.

"Thanks," Drake said. "Getting hit by that would have really put a damper on my day."

Allie rubbed her hands together to brush away some dirt. "Well, we're not getting over that way. Perhaps there's a way through the jungle?"

Allie, Geneva, and Ingrid started exploring the area while Drake stepped back from the wall and surveyed the surroundings. Without saying anything to anyone, he let his eyes wander the terrain. Then, with all the agility of a chimpanzee attempting to balance a bucket of ice cream on its head, Drake pulled himself onto the lowest branch of a century-old beech tree and slowly moved from branch to branch until he positioned himself on a limb directly overhanging the wall.

"Hey, it's a building of some sort," Drake said, calling down to his friends.

"Drake! Come down here!" Geneva hollered. "You're going to fall and break something."

"Yes, mom," Drake sighed. He took a step toward the trunk.

"Wait," Allie said. "Before you come down, tell us what you see."

Drake shifted his feet to get a better look. "It looks like this was a structure at one point. Directly across from me, it looks like there was a door, which is blocked by a log. I can also guess those are remnants of a fireplace, a window, and a rusty lawn chair with no seat."

"How can you see all that?" Geneva asked.

"Unlike the exterior landscaping, the inside is mostly dirt with a few random clumps of grass. I'm going to go down to take a closer look."

"Drake, don't do anything stupid," Geneva said. "Get back

here."

Drake grinned down from the tree, just like the Cheshire Cat. "Don't worry. I specialize in stupid."

As the women watched, Drake crouched, wrapped his arms around the branch he stood on, and dropped. As he moved farther away from the trunk, the branch narrowed and started to bend precariously.

"Drake,"

Before Geneva had a chance to finish her sentence, the branch, unable to hold Drake's weight any longer, snapped, and he dropped from sight.

"Drake!" Geneva yelled.

He didn't answer.

"Drake?" Geneva asked, with more genuine concern in her voice than anger.

There was another pause, then he finally answered. "I'm okay. I landed funny and got the wind knocked out of me."

"How are you going to get back?" Geneva asked.

"I'll worry about that in a bit. I'm going to look around first. Give me a few minutes. Entertain yourselves for a little while. Read a book or something."

Allie and Ingrid found a comfortable-enough patch of grass to sit on, while Geneva paced back and forth along the wall like an expectant father. Geneva checked the time and wondered how long it had been since Drake had responded to her. Five minutes? Ten? She glanced at her friends and saw Allie was attempting to make a paper airplane from a large leaf, and Ingrid's eyes were closed as if she were deep in meditation. Not able to take the silence anymore, Geneva stepped up to the wall.

"Drake?" she called.

Although Geneva caught the attention of Ingrid and Allie, who both looked up at her, she didn't hear a peep from Drake.

"Drake!" Geneva screamed, loud enough to disturb a group of resting blackbirds and causing them to take wing.

"What?" Drake asked from behind her.

Geneva spun around and spotted Drake, who had appeared as if by magic. "Where did you come from?"

Drake cocked a thumb in the direction they'd all come from originally. "There was a hole in the wall large enough for me to fit through on the opposite wall. There was a path there that led me back to the park, then I simply followed our own footsteps to here."

"Did you find anything?" Allie asked as she tossed aside the leaf she'd been messing with, got to her feet, and brushed away the dirt from her backside.

"This," Drake said, holding up a small tin box, a twin to the one Geneva found. He shook the box, and something inside rattled. "Underneath the fireplace was a hole covered by a stone with an etching on it that looked similar to that coin that you found. I took a picture of it. I'll show it to you when we get back to the hotel. Come on. Let's go find someone with a soldering iron."

* * *

Asger Berg didn't dress for the weather or for comfort, but rather for concealment. He'd worn blue jeans, a battered pair of Nike running shoes, a sweatshirt with a hood over his head, and sunglasses. He figured he looked like the world's worst spy, but he also figured that people wouldn't take a second look at him and based on the interaction of everyone he passed in the park, he realized he was right.

Asger had properly assumed that Ingrid and her friends would check out the park after he'd given them the clue. Since it was Saturday and he didn't have to work, Asger set out for the park before dawn, and when he arrived, the park was still quiet, and the dew still clung to the grass as he made his way to the monument itself. There, he paused before the stark, modernist sculpture commemorating the resistance fighters who the Nazis had executed on the spot.

"Beneath the fallen," Asger murmured, recalling the coded message. "Could it really be at this exact spot?"

His thoughts turned to all the artifacts that had gone missing during the war. There were countless pieces of jewelry, coins, art, sculptures and more that disappeared when the Nazis invaded and took whatever they desired as they spread across Denmark like a blight.

Asger made a complete circle around the memorial, searching for anything that might be out of place, but didn't find anything of significance. From there, he checked the nearby sites and read all the signs to see if they might provide any clue as to where someone would hide an eighty-year-old secret. When that failed, as a backup plan, he retreated away from the memorial section of the park, found a bench to sit on, and waited for Ingrid to arrive.

When her party finally did, Asger watched as they investigated all the same places he had. Then, as he spied on them, they came together, had a brief discussion, and headed off to the edge of the park.

Asger kept an eye on them, and as the last person disappeared into the woods bordering the park, he jumped from the bench and ran across the grass until he came to within a few yards of the spot where they'd entered. Once there, he slowed and opted for stealth instead of speed as he entered the woods, trying not to make any sounds that would give his presence away. When he saw the group stop at the foundation of the ancient farmhouse, his heart skipped a beat.

Asger had spent many summer days inside the relic, as had most of the children in the area. Little kids who liked to play in the woods used the house as a fort, or a base of operations when they pretended to be the Lost Boys in Peter Pan, or the jungle home as Tarzan. Teenagers often visited the house to do the things that teenagers do, and couples often used it as a place for an erotic rendezvous spot. The thought that he'd been in that place so often and it might be the location of a real hidden treasure made the hair on the back of his neck stand up.

Asger stepped off the main trail and concealed himself behind a wide tree. From there, he watched the man climb a tree, then drop into the house. After several minutes, Asger heard someone enter the woods from behind him. He crouched and froze, hoping not to be seen, and held his breath when the man passed by no more than four feet away. Asger stayed in his position, peering through the gaps in bushes and watched as the man showed a metal box to the others. He eavesdropped on the conversation, then stayed still when the group left the area. He counted to twenty in his head and followed them out of the woods. Asger paused at the edge, still concealed by the trees, and noticed the group was hurrying to the parking area. Realizing he'd lose his quarry if he didn't move quickly, he stepped forward, caught his foot on a root, and toppled over. He threw his arms out in front of him and managed to get his hands into position before hitting the earth. A stinging sensation ran up both arms right to his shoulders, and he landed face first into a mud puddle. When he got to his knees, he took a moment to assess his condition. First, he removed the sunglasses, noticing one of the cheap plastic lenses had a crack from top to bottom, grateful it wasn't an eyeball that had hit whatever the eyewear had. He closed the glasses and shoved them into the front pocket of his sweatshirt. He wiggled his fingers, made sure his elbows were operational, then put both arms in the air and pinwheeled them. Satisfied he'd not sustained an injury that required medical attention, Asger got to his feet. He looked toward the parking lot and discovered Ingrid was no longer in sight.

"Shit," Asger said.

As Asger trudged back to his car, his mind turned to his colleague, Mette. She was sharp, discreet, and had contacts in both the archeological and local history communities that could prove invaluable. As to whether he could trust her, he didn't know, but he was certain he should confide in Mette and enlist her help. Together, perhaps they could solve a mystery and bring a lost piece of history back into the light.

When he returned to his car, he unlocked and opened the door, then took off his sweatshirt, turning it inside-out in the process to avoid transferring mud to the interior of his Volkswagen. He searched in his glove box for napkins, and, finding a handful, he wiped the mud from his face before tossing the napkins into the floorboard of the passenger seat.

Asger took a few minutes to rehearse what he wanted to say to Mette countless times, then picked his cell from his back pocket. With a mixture of nervousness and determination, he called her. The phone rang half a dozen times before she finally picked up.

"Hello?"

"Mette? It's Asger. Do you have a moment? There's something I need to discuss with you."

There was a brief pause on the other end of the line. "Of course, Asger. Is everything all right?"

Asger took a deep breath, then told Mette everything that had happened so far, from the coded messages in the photograph, to his attempt to find the treasure, to his childhood friend swooping in and discovering something that had been literally within arm's reach since he was a boy.

"So? What does it all mean?" Mette asked.

"I believe that whatever they found might lead to a hidden cache of World War II artifacts or treasures buried somewhere around here."

"Treasure?" Mette said, the tone of her voice changing from skepticism to fascination.

Asger took a breath and laid it all out on the table, and when he finished, she was silent for a long moment, as if processing what she had heard.

"Asger, this is… an incredible story, but how do you know your friend is even on the trail of something that fantastic? But I have to admit, if you're right, this could be one of the most significant historical find in decades."

"Yes, that's what I'm trying to tell you," Asger said. "And I'm sure I can find out what she found. I'm certain that won't take more than a simple phone call to express my interest. She came to me, after all."

"Fine, fine," Mette said. "You need to remember that this could turn out to be risky. Have you considered the legal implications? The potential danger?"

Asger thought about the points for only a moment. "I have. That's why I'm coming to you. I need your help, Mette. Your expertise, your contacts. But I don't want to go through any official channels, at least not until I find out if Ingrid truly has something worth pursuing."

Mette paused. "It's a lot to ask, Asger. We could both lose our jobs if this goes wrong, but, if you're right, it would be a discovery of a lifetime. Okay. I'm in. I'll help you, but first you need to find out what your friend has and if it's worth my time."

Relief washed over Asger. He hadn't realized how much he had been counting on Mette's support. "Thank you," he said. "I promise we'll be careful. We'll do this right, and before I bring you in any further, I'll determine if there is anything to find, or if this is just a part of the game she's playing."

"Good," Mette said. "I'll see you at the museum on Monday."

Mette clicked off the phone without saying anything, leaving Asger waiting for another word that never came. After almost a full minute, he took the phone from his ear, looked at it, then ended the call and dropped it onto the passenger seat.

Asger leaned forward to start the car, then sat back and retrieved his phone. He went through the previous call logs to find Ingrid's number and was about to push the green button to connect but stopped when he saw a streak of dirt on his hand. Once again, he put the phone to the side and looked at himself in the rearview mirror. Although the destroyed sunglasses and his hoodie had caught much of the mud, he still wore streaks of dirt down his cheeks and across his chin like he was preparing himself for battle. Knowing he needed to clean up and change before reengaging with Ingrid, fully expecting her to invite him over, he started his Volkswagen and headed home for a shower and a fresh shirt.

CHAPTER FOUR

"Are you sure you're doing that right?" Allie asked.

Drake looked up from the delicate tin box, soldering iron in hand, and threw Allie a glare. "Of course. All I need to do is melt the bead, and the box should slip right open. I watched the guy do the last one, and it only took him a minute or so."

"Just one more follow-up question. Was he wearing no safety equipment and performing the task on the bathroom counter of a hotel?"

Drake glanced down at his work surface. Beneath the tin was the exposed granite countertop. "Good point," he said, picking up the box. "Put a towel down."

Allie rolled her eyes but still grabbed a towel from the bar and laid it flat on the sink.

"Thanks," Drake said as he set the tin in the center. "At least if something goes horribly wrong, we only need to pay for a towel. Please take a step back."

Allie complied by taking a seat on the side of the bathtub next to Geneva. Ingrid sat on the closed toilet lid, the most comfortable seat in the crowded room.

"Everyone ready?" Drake asked.

Not expecting an answer, Drake tightened his grip on the soldering iron, crouched, and, beginning at the corner, slowly ran the iron along the side. As he did, a whisper of smoke drifted lazily into the air, and a hushed hiss was the only sound in the room.

It took over a minute for him to do one side of the box, and as he gained confidence in his technique, he sped up.

"Hand me a few tissues, will you?" Drake asked Ingrid.

Ingrid leaned over, plucked a few from the box, and handed them to Drake. He used them to grasp the bottom of the box and tipped it on his side. At first the lid didn't budge, but he noticed a bead of solder had set. With a short bit of exposure to the hot iron, the bead melted, and the lid fell free.

"There. That was easy," Drake said, setting the iron in its holder and unplugging it for good measure.

"What's in there?" Geneva asked.

"Let's give it a couple of minutes to cool, and we'll find out," Drake said. "In the meantime, do any of you have any good jokes?"

Allie rolled her eyes, causing Drake to grin.

"Okay, then," Drake said. "I got one. Why did the lobster blush?" He paused, hoping to get a guess, but he recognized no one was willing to speak. Geneva was already rolling her eyes at him. "Because it saw the ocean's bottom!"

Drake guffawed while Geneva rolled her eyes again. Ingrid stared at the floor, and Allie shook her head.

"Come on, Drake. Just open the box," Allie said.

Drake shrugged. "Some people just don't realize good comedy when they hear it."

"Or," Allie said, "perhaps some people don't tell good jokes."

Drake stuck his tongue out at her. "Sorry. You come up with a bad one next time. Let's see what's in here." He tipped the box upside down and lifted it from the counter. On top of the hotel towel was a coin and a parchment, two inches long, rolled tightly and tied with a short piece of twine.

"This looks familiar," Drake said as he picked up the coin and held it in the air, the light glinting off its surface.

Geneva left the room and returned a moment later with the coin she'd discovered earlier. She placed it on the towel, and Drake set the one in his hand next to hers.

"Looks like a match to me," Geneva said. "Although neither one is perfectly round, the markings match."

"Flip them over," Allie said.

Drake did as requested. All four peered at the coins. Both coins featured a Viking longship on one side, but the obverse had different symbols. One featured a sea serpent, the other looked like the sunrise over the ocean.

"What do you suppose those differences mean?" Allie asked. Drake shook his head. "Don't know. Are they differences in value? It's hard to say."

"I'll bet Asger would know," Ingrid said.

"Maybe you should call him later," Geneva said.

"Are you sure?" Ingrid asked. "You don't think he'll question why I keep asking him about little trinkets that we keep stumbling across?"

"Why not? He's your friend. You trust him, don't you?"

"Of course," Ingrid said.

Geneva nodded. "That's good enough for me. What's on the paper?"

Drake moved the coins aside and picked up the paper and carefully undid the knotted twine. As the parchment unrolled, five lines of symbols appeared.

"Looks like a cipher of some sort," Drake said. "Do we know anyone who is good at these?"

Geneva smiled. "You mean besides Allie and Ingrid, the puzzle twins?"

"Yeah, exactly," Drake said.

Allie stepped over to Drake's side. "Hold that steady."

Drake unrolled the parchment completely and held it tight while Allie snapped a picture with her phone.

"Come on, Ingrid. Let's give these two some quiet time," Allie said.

"In the bathroom?" Ingrid snickered. "Gross."

Allie left the room with Ingrid a step behind her. Together, they moved to the desk and, using her photo as a reference, copied the images from the phone to a pad of hotel stationery. Once done, she made a copy and handed one to Ingrid.

"Let's see if we can crack this," Allie said.

Allie put her head down, and for several minutes worked on the puzzle. Exasperated, she marked a big 'X' across the page and wrote the original sequence on a fresh piece of paper and tried again. Instead of diving right in, Allie stared at the sheet, trying to determine where to go first. When trying to solve a substitution cipher, she always started by looking for patterns in the text, like common letters and letter groups, but in this case, she felt like a toddler looking at the English alphabet for the first time.

Allie felt someone behind her and caught the scent of Ingrid's soap when Ingrid leaned over her and gave her a hug.

"Sorry. I can't break this," Allie said.

Ingrid squeezed her a little tighter. "It's okay. You didn't have much of a chance."

"Why is that?" Allie asked, her tone terse. "I've solved plenty of ciphers."

"True. But never one in Danish," Ingrid said. Ingrid kissed the top of Allie's head and placed her paper on the desk. She gave Allie another squeeze and let her go as Allie picked up the paper. She studied the note for a moment, then shook her head. She had been taking lessons in the language but didn't recognize any of the words on the page.

"What does this mean?" Allie asked.

Before Ingrid could answer, there was a knock on the door.

"I got it," Geneva said, rising from the bed where she'd been paging through a local travel magazine while she waited for her friends to decipher the clue. She sauntered to the door and looked through the peephole. "It's your friend."

"Asger?" Ingrid said.

"Yeah. He must have come right over when you called him."

Ingrid rose and stepped to the door. "I didn't call him yet."

Geneva stepped away from the door, giving her friend some room. "Lucky coincidence then."

Ingrid opened the door. "Asger. What brings you here?"

Asger forced a smile. "I was on my way home and remembered you were staying here. Since I rarely get to see you, I thought I'd take a chance and see if you were in."

Ingrid hesitated.

"You are going to invite me in, aren't you?" Asger asked, taking a step toward the door.

Ingrid hesitated a second time. "Of course." She stepped backward and opened the door wide for her friend. "Please, come in. Geneva, you know, but let me introduce you to Allie and Drake."

Asger shook hands with each person as Ingrid made the introductions. "How are you enjoying Denmark?"

"It's pretty here," Allie said.

Asger smiled. "It is, indeed. I'm not sure why Ingrid ever left home."

"It wasn't me. My parents emigrated. I'm an American."

"Oh, not at all. You are truly a daughter of Denmark."

"Ingrid, ask him about the coins," Drake said.

"He can hear you, you know," Ingrid said.

"Coins?" Asger said.

Geneva held out her hand and opened it. "These."

Asger looked at the disks in her palm. "May I?"

Geneva nodded, then dropped them into Asger's hand.

He held them up. Unable to see them clearly, he moved to the desk and placed them under the desk light.

"This one I've seen before, yes?" Asger said, pointing at the coin on the right.

Geneva nodded. "Yes."

"Where did you find this other one?"

Everyone waited for everyone else to answer. When she realized the silence had reached an almost uncomfortable level, Ingrid spoke up. "In a geocache."

Asger looked her in the eyes for a moment and then turned his attention back to the coins. "Is it often you find such… things of value in geocaches?"

"Not often, but it happens occasionally," Drake said, rising from the edge of the bed. "Usually, cache owners leave them as prizes for the people who are the first finders of the geocache. Isn't that right, Geneva?"

"Yes," she said without missing a beat. "I found a gift certificate worth over a hundred dollars once as a prize, and Ingrid found a silver coin. Remember that, Ingrid?"

Ingrid nodded. "Yes. So, it's unusual to find valuable items, but it does happen."

"Hmm," Asger said, seemingly satisfied. "Did you have a question about these?"

Ingrid looked into his palm and turned them over. "The backs. What's the significance of the patterns?"

Asger leaned in for a closer look.

"Drake thought perhaps they represented different values. Like the sunrise was worth more than the snake."

It was Asger's time for silence as he studied the coins for almost a minute. "Yes. I believe Drake is correct, but my expertise isn't with coins. Do you mind if I take a photograph of them and ask a colleague at the museum about them?"

Ingrid looked at her party. "What do you think?"

Drake nodded, Allie remained silent.

"Go ahead," Geneva said.

Asger placed the coins on the desk and removed his phone from his pocket. He took several pictures of the coins, including both sides, the edges, close-ups and shots from a few inches away. He snapped one last picture, slid his phone back into his pocket, and picked up the coins.

"Thank you," he said to Geneva as he handed her the coins. "I'll ask around on Monday and if I can find anything out, I will send a text to Ingrid." Asger looked up and spotted the red digits on the clock next to the bed. "Oh, I need to run. I'm meeting someone, and I'm already late."

"Oh, well, thank you for stopping by," Ingrid said, following Asger as he moved to the door and opened it.

"I'll text you just as soon as I find something out about the coins," Asger said. "And perhaps you and your friends will join me for dinner before you leave Copenhagen?"

Ingrid smiled. "That would be nice. We'd enjoy that."

Asger gave one nod, then turned and headed down the hallway. Ingrid watched him until he turned the corner leading to the lobby and shut the door. She engaged the security locks on the door, then rejoined her friends.

"That was nice of him to drop in and say hello," Allie said, picking up the cipher Ingrid had busted. "Now that he's gone, can you translate this for us?"

"Of course," Ingrid said. She moved to Allie and took the paper from her hand. "Sun and sea weathers hull and sail. Time claims the greatest of kings. Spires stretch toward the sky. Monarchs lay entombed inside. Let the runes be your guide."

Drake nodded. "Poetic. But what does it mean?"

"Give me a minute," Ingrid said. "If I'm right, we need to take a little road trip."

Drake grinned. "Oh. I love going on a good road trip. I hope there will be snacks!"

Ingrid laughed. "Give me a few minutes and then we'll see about the snacks."

Ingrid took the piece of paper, studied it for a second, and then began performing research on her phone. She spotted something of interest, found a blank sheet of paper, and jotted a note. She spent a few moments scanning a different web page, then added additional notes to the paper. While she worked, the other three crowded around the desk, watching, but not interrupting.

Ingrid scrolled on the phone for another ten minutes, and in that time, only placed an asterisk next to one entry on her sheet. Satisfied she'd done all she could for the moment, Ingrid closed all the browser windows and set her phone on the desk.

"Well? What did you learn?" Geneva asked after no one spoke for an extended ten seconds.

"Yeah," Drake added. "Road trip or not?"

Ingrid picked up her notes and held them out for Drake to read. He stared at them for a moment.

"Anyone ever tell you that you write like a doctor who specializes in stenography?" Drake asked.

Ingrid smiled. "Actually, yes. In a nutshell, we need to go to a church in Roskilde to find Harald Bluetooth."

"Bluetooth? The wireless tech guy?" Drake asked.

"Close, but no," Ingrid said. "Harald Bluetooth was the king of Denmark in the mid-to-late nine hundreds. He is best known for introducing Christianity to Denmark. Interesting fun fact, though, the Bluetooth logo comes from the king's initials represented as runes."

"That is a fun fact. Why the name? Did Bluetooth really have a blue tooth?" Drake asked.

"Unknown," Ingrid said. "Tradition says the name came from him having a rotten tooth that appeared dark blue, but there's no actual evidence of it. His real name was Harald Gormsson, which means 'son of Gorm', who was the king before

Bluetooth."

"Oh, another fun fact, Harald Bluetooth, introduced the first nationwide coinage in Denmark."

Geneva went into her pocket, retrieved the two coins, and dropped them in Ingrid's hand. "Like these?"

Ingrid shrugged. "I don't know. I'm not a coin person, except what's in the little cubby in my car door."

Drake plucked a coin from her palm and studied it. "Can I borrow your phone?"

Without a verbal answer, Ingrid unlocked her screen and handed it to him.

Drake set the coin flat on the desk, brought up the camera, and took a picture.

"How far is Roskilde from here?" Allie asked.

"Not far. Less than an hour, depending on traffic," Ingrid answered.

"The blue tooth guy is on this coin," Drake said.

"What?" Allie said.

"Look." Drake set the phone on the desk so everyone could see the image. "Right there."

"Where?" Geneva asked. "All I see is a snake head."

Drake expanded the image, then pointed at the snake's eye with the tip of Ingrid's pen.

Geneva finally spotted it. "I mean, it could be. Or maybe it's a case of seeing things because our brain is filling in information, like picking shapes out of the clouds."

"Okay. Good point. Give me the other coin."

Drake took the coin, took a picture, then studied the second image. "Yep. There's one here, too."

Once again, he set down the phone, enlarged the image, and pointed it out. The sunrise on the coin displayed rays that disappeared into the ocean, but in a spot where the vertical rays met the horizontal waves was the Bluetooth symbol.

"Okay, I'm a believer," Geneva said. "Do you think these

coins come from around Bluetooth's time, and if so, why did your friend say they were worth practically nothing?"

Ingrid shook her head. "I don't know. I'm certainly not going to press the issue with him. If need be, we can find another coin expert to examine them."

"Besides," Allie added, "they might not even be authentic, and merely like tokens."

"Like getting the crushed penny at the zoo with the gorilla on it," Drake said.

"Right," Allie said. "Although I always went for the elephant. I love elephants. We should go to Africa someday so I can see the elephants."

Drake hesitated. "Sounds good to me. Everyone, clear your schedules for next summer."

"Should we go to the church now? We can talk about next year in the car." Geneva asked.

"Good idea," Allie said.

"Hold on," Ingrid said. "Before we go, I should tell you that there's a chance Bluetooth isn't there. According to historical accounts, what they presume as his actual burial site got discovered in Poland a few years ago."

"When?" Drake asked.

"2022."

"No problem, let's go," Drake said. "Whoever hid these items did so way before 2022, so even if Bluetooth isn't in Roskilde, whoever stashed the stuff thought he was."

Geneva smiled and kissed Drake on the forehead. "Such a clever detective."

Ingrid picked up her phone and grabbed the keys to the rental car. "Let's ride."

Asger watched from his car as the group climbed into their rental car, with Ingrid behind the wheel. He sat up straight in his seat and held his phone up.

"You were right. They're leaving."

On the video call, Mette sighed. "Such as I guessed."

"I don't know why you want me to follow them," Asger argued. "I'm more than capable of figuring out this riddle myself. You realize I have photos of Ingrid's notes and the coins they have."

"That may be true, but do it anyway. Follow them wherever they go. Whatever it is they find, and I don't care if it turns out to be as insignificant as a button, I want you to report it back to me."

Asger didn't respond.

"Did you hear me?" Mette asked.

Before Asger could answer, he picked up a series of rapid clicks. Thinking he lost the call, he looked at the display where Mette appeared frozen.

"Mette? Are you still there?"

"Yes. Do you understand what I want from you?"

"Follow them. But what about my work at the museum? Who knows how long I'll be away? Won't anyone notice that I'm not there?"

Mette thought for a moment. "Don't worry. I'll take care of your time sheet and put a note on your calendar that you're out in the field for the week. If this lasts longer than that, I'll adjust things as we go. Speaking of going, you're wasting time."

Mette disconnected the call. Asger dropped his phone into the passenger seat, started the engine, and hoped he wasn't too far behind his quarry.

CHAPTER FIVE

Just under an hour later, Ingrid parallel-parked across the street from the Roskilde Cathedral and the group exited the SUV, rushed across the road, and moved toward the front door.

"We need to hurry. They close in a half-hour," Ingrid said, pointing to the sign on the front of the massive oak door.

The group entered, paid the small admission fee, and Allie grabbed a map of the building. She studied it for a moment and passed it to Ingrid. "I don't see Bluetooth on here," she said as Ingrid took the paper from her.

Ingrid looked over the map for a moment. When she looked up, she spotted a tour guide and approached her.

"Excuse me, Kat," Ingrid said, reading the young woman's name tag while pointing at the map. "Can you tell me where in here they buried Harald Bluetooth?"

"I hate to disappoint you, but there's a chance he's not here at all," Kat answered. The woman pulled a pen from the pocket of the red blazer she wore. "Bluetooth got buried in the Trinity Church, which he had built after he named Roskilde as the new capital of Denmark and moved here from Jelling, where he also built a church. When he died in 986, they brought him back here from Jomsborg, which is in Poland. They tore down Trinity Church in 1026, and they built a new cathedral on that site. Over time, it grew into what you're standing in now."

"Did they move Bluetooth's body?" Allie asked. "Is it here in the cathedral?"

Kat shrugged. "History says he lies within the northwestern pier of the apse, but they never found a grave or remains of any kind there. He has a pillar tomb over near the sarcophagus of Queen Louise, right here." Kat pointed at the location with her pen. "I'd walk you over there myself, but we're closing in a few minutes, and I need to begin ushering people from the building."

"I understand. Thank you," Ingrid said. "We will only be a couple of minutes. The stories of Harald Bluetooth fascinate my friend here and she always wanted to visit his burial spot."

Kat shrugged. "You might need to go to Poland for that, I hear. Go on. If you're not done by the time we close, I'll get you last to afford you a few extra minutes."

Ingrid thanked her again and referenced the map and began speed-walking through the cathedral.

"It's beautiful in here," Geneva said as they passed through the building, which featured a blend of architectural styles which reflected its evolution over the centuries.

They didn't stop to admire any of the medieval frescoes, ornate sarcophagi, any of the tombs or chapels, or any of the historical items held within. Instead, with little time available, Ingrid took them right to the correct area, and a few seconds later, they spotted the pillar of Harald Bluetooth. The fresco looked fresh and featured the king wearing a red shirt covered with a gold vest, along with a blue skirt, red tights and shoes. He held a scepter in one hand, an orb in the other. Above him was a woman holding a decapitated head. To his right floated a cherub. Instead of a traditional crown on his head, he wore a white hat with a gold crown atop that.

"This is interesting. Whose head is that woman holding?" Drake asked.

"I'll ask on the way out. For now, see what you can," Ingrid said.

The group worked as one, inspecting the fresco for some sort of sign or something that didn't quite belong.

Geneva stepped to the side and glanced down the length of the corridor. "She's coming for us. If you're going to do something, make it snappy."

"Snappy!" Drake said. "Everyone should take pictures, and we can analyze them when we leave. If we don't find anything, we can come back tomorrow."

"Good idea, Drake," Allie said as she pulled her phone from her back pocket.

While Drake, Allie, and Ingrid took pictures, Geneva monitored Kat's progress.

"Hurry up. She's only twenty feet away," Geneva said.

Kat turned the corner the moment the friends finished taking photos. "I'm sorry, but we're closing for the day. Since you came in so late, I'd be happy to honor your entry tickets for tomorrow as well."

"Thanks, we'd like that. There's a lot in here we didn't get to view," Ingrid said.

Kat led the group to the entrance and gave them each a pass for the following day. "I'll see you tomorrow."

Ingrid was the last person ushered out the door, and the second she left, a woman in a dark blue suit approached her.

"Ingrid Snyder?" the woman asked.

"Yes. Who are you?"

The woman reached into a pocket and held out identification. "I am Inspector Louise Jensen. I'm with the Politiet."

"Isn't that the national police force?" Ingrid asked.

"It is."

"What can I do for you?" Ingrid asked.

Inspector Jensen pocketed her ID, removed her sunglasses, and ran a hand through her short brown hair. "Perhaps I could have a moment of your time?" She cocked her head toward Ingrid's friends.

Ingrid removed the car keys from her pocket and passed them to Drake, who was standing closest to her. "Why don't you guys meet me at the car? I'll be there in a couple of minutes. Right, Inspector?"

The cop nodded.

Drake hesitated and turned toward the street. "Come on, ladies."

The inspector waited until the trio had crossed the street and turned her attention back to Ingrid. "Can you tell me what you're doing here?"

"Checking out the church," Ingrid said.

Jensen's brow furrowed as she looked at Ingrid, waiting for more information that didn't come. "I meant, what are you doing in the country?"

"Visiting with friends."

"You're an American."

It surprised Ingrid to find that the inspector knew that, but she didn't let it show. "So what?"

"You're off the beaten tourism path for an American."

"I'm Danish. I was born in American, but both of my parents are from here. They have dual citizenship. They used to bring me here all the time when I was young, and I thought it would make for a fun trip for my friends and I."

"If you're on a holiday, then why are you hunting for something?"

"What do you mean?"

"Someone observed you, thought it suspicious, and reported you. My division has been following you."

Ingrid frowned. "I'm sorry. I don't understand. Which

division are you in?"

"Stolen antiquities."

Ingrid hesitated for a second and laughed. "You think we're treasure hunters? No. We're merely here on a geocaching trip."

It was the inspector's turn to look confused.

"Geocaching is an activity that's like a modern-day treasure hunt. We use GPS devices to find things that other players have hidden."

"What kind of treasures?" Inspector Jensen asked.

Ingrid pulled her phone from her back pocket and brought up her geocaching app and switched the screen to the live map.

"Look here," Ingrid said. "These are all the geocaches in the immediate area. Follow me and we'll find one."

Ingrid checked the map and strolled a hundred feet up the street with Inspector Jensen a half of a step behind her. Ingrid stopped at a 'No Parking' sign, checked behind it, and produced a tiny magnetic container.

"What's that?" Inspector Jensen asked.

"We call it a nano." Ingrid unscrewed the top, tipped it over, and dropped a piece of paper into the inspector's hand.

"What's this?"

"A log. Every geocache contains one. I would add my name to that paper, put it back together, and put it back where I found it. Then I would log it in my app that I found it."

Inspector Jensen stared at the paper for a moment and handed it back to Ingrid. "This is what you're doing? Going around and putting your name on paper?"

"You got it."

"I believe it's silly, but it's not against the law." Inspector Jensen said.

"What made you assume we were doing anything illegal?"

"Like I said, someone called in a report, a report that I'm going to close when I get back to the station. A warning for you, though. If someone called this in once, it may happen again. I'll give you my card, and if anyone else hassles you, call and let me know."

The inspector produced a business card like it was a magic trick and placed it in Ingrid's hand.

"I will. Thank you," Ingrid said.

Inspector Jensen nodded, turned around, and walked away.

"What was that about?" Allie asked as Ingrid approached the car.

"Typical LEO encounter," Ingrid said. Many geocachers had encounters with Law Enforcement Officers at one time or another. If the cops were familiar with geocaching, the meeting was typically a brief one. Otherwise, it usually took a few minutes to explain why someone was rooting around in the bushes or looking under light pole skirts.

"Why did she only want to talk to you? How did she know your name?" Allie asked.

Ingrid shrugged. "I don't know, and I didn't ask. Did you find out anything while I was gone?"

"Actually, it's Drake to the rescue again," Geneva said.

Drake moved to Ingrid's side. "I found the Bluetooth symbol in the king's crown. It looks like there's other runes there, but I can't make them out. Take a look."

Ingrid glanced at the screen, then asked for paper and pen. Once she had them in hand, she drew what she saw in the photos, then used her phone to decipher what they meant. In all, the process took just under five minutes. "Home. Stone."

"Does that mean anything to you?" Drake asked.

"I guess it means in the morning we need to go to Jelling."

* * *

"Wake up sleepyheads. We're almost there."

Ingrid looked into the mirror and spotted both Geneva and Drake looking at her from the back seat. They'd been on the road for almost three hours, and if history was any sort of indicator, at least Drake would be asleep, bored with watching the scenery change. She smiled, then turned her attention back to the road just in time to spot the parking lot she needed. When she turned off the car, the doors unlocked, and everyone stepped onto the asphalt.

"Which way?" Geneva asked.

"There," Ingrid said as she pointed toward an unassuming white church.

"Are we looking for another grave?" Drake asked.

"Even easier. We need to look at the runestones."

"What are runestones?"

Ingrid stopped for a moment, took off her sunglasses, and brushed away a runaway strand of her red hair that flew into her face. She wrangled it back into her ponytail, then put her glasses on. "They are two large stones into which carvings were done. There's a smaller one that was raised by King Gorm in memory of his wife. The bigger one Harald Bluetooth raised in memory of his parents."

"You believe we'll find a clue on the stones?" Allie asked.

"Yes. If I interpreted the clues in Roskilde correctly. Let's go find out."

Together, the group walked along a cobblestone path until they came to a wrought-iron gate that allowed them entry into the graveyard. Ingrid, taking the lead, moved past the well-maintained graves and toward the church. She stopped when they arrived at the runestones.

"I hope we don't need to get too close to them," Drake said.

"I don't get it. They weren't like this when I was here last," Ingrid said.

Ingrid stepped closer and inspected the housing that protected the stones. Each stone was surrounded by a cage comprising a solid side and roof, and three sides in a thick glass. "I remember coming here as a girl and touching those."

"I guess we can't do that anymore," Allie said. "Is there another way we can see the markings? Use our phones again, maybe?"

Ingrid shrugged. "Why not? I don't think we have another choice."

"Which one is Bluetooth's?" Geneva asked.

"The taller one," Ingrid said, pointing to the stone that stood over seven feet tall and weighed in at ten tons. "If there's something there, it will be on that one."

Ingrid, Allie, and Geneva each selected an open window through which they could take pictures of the stone while Drake moved to each, inserting his help where he could.

Drake was next to Geneva at the back window when he took two steps backward to get the entire stone in the frame.

"Geneva, could you step to the side for a minute while I take this picture?"

Geneva looked at him, then moved out of the frame. Drake, not having the massive stone in his view, took another step back.

"Drake, watch it!" Geneva warned.

He turned his attention to his girlfriend, but as he shuffled back another half-step, he stepped into the hedge lining the graveyard. He pinwheeled his arms for balance, almost caught it, then tumbled backward, falling over the two-foot-tall hedge and landing flat on his butt.

"Drake!" Geneva screamed as she ran to him. It took a minute to make her way to him since she elected to use the sidewalk instead of attempting a jump over the hedge herself, but when she got there, she found Drake still lying on his back, eyes closed, both lower legs tangled in the brush.

"Drake?" Geneva said as she got closer. She knelt beside him and gently touched his cheek with her fingertips.

Drake groaned.

"Drake?"

"What happened?" Allie asked.

"He tripped over the hedge."

"Did he hit his head?"

"Geneva," Drake whispered.

"Yes? Are you okay?"

"Come closer."

Geneva leaned in to hear him better. Drake responded by opening his eyes, throwing his arms around her, and bringing her in for a kiss. Startled at first, she relaxed and enjoyed the smooch. When they broke contact, Geneva got back to her feet.

"Are you okay?" Allie asked.

"I think so." Drake tried to lift his legs but couldn't. "Nope. I'm stuck."

"Hold on," Geneva said. She stepped over his prone body and moved close to the hedge and grabbed his right leg while Allie positioned herself on the left. Gently, Geneva wrestled Drake's leg free and held it up while Allie freed the other.

"You've got a nasty scratch here," Allie said. "We should check if there's a restroom nearby, so you can clean it up."

"Okay, thanks. Let me go."

The women released his legs, and Drake brought them back to his chest and rolled onto his side. He lay still for a few seconds, then held his hand up. "Anyone find my phone?"

Geneva and Allie scoured the area for it, and when Allie found it leaning up against a headstone, she retrieved it and dropped it in his hand.

"Thanks." Drake rolled over more, almost on his stomach, then took a couple of pictures and handed the phone back to Allie. "Pass that to Ingrid and see if she can read it."

As Allie passed the phone, Drake got to his feet, brushed himself off, and lifted his pant leg to check the damage. Sure enough, he was still bleeding.

"I'm going into the church to see if they have a restroom." Drake said.

When Drake left the area, Geneva and Allie crowded around

Ingrid. Ingrid looked at the message for less than a minute.

"Tree beyond. Elias 1610," Ingrid said.

"And?" Geneva asked.

"That's it. It was another substitution cipher. I think we need to search for an Elias somewhere in this cemetery who either died or was born in 1610," Ingrid said.

"Seems like an easy enough task," Allie said. "There looks to be only a couple of hundred headstones here."

Ingrid sighed. "I wish I shared your confidence and enthusiasm."

Geneva looked around them. The graveyard looked well-maintained and separated into small plots, each one bordered by a short hedge exactly like the one Drake had tripped over. "I think if we each took a section; we could breeze through this pretty quickly."

The friends agreed, and each one took off in a different direction. Geneva was correct. Since they'd laid out the graveyard so well, it was but a matter of walking along the gravel paths, reading the names on the headstones as they went.

Twenty minutes later, in the far northeast corner of the graveyard, Allie made the find.

"Over here!" she yelled as she waved her arms to attract not only the attention of her friends, but also other visitors to the UNESCO World Heritage Site. When Ingrid, Geneva, and Drake clustered around her, she pointed at the faded gray stone that declared Elias had died in 1610, just short of his fiftieth birthday. "So now what?"

"We need to find the tree beyond," Ingrid said.

"That should be easy enough. There's a cluster over there at the bottom of that little hill," Drake said, pointing to a copse fifty yards away.

"That's a burial mound," Ingrid said. "You're right. If it's in a tree, it would be one of those."

The four left the graveyard, waited for a half-dozen bikers

to pass on a trail before them, then hiked to the tree. The oak tree stood before them, at least thirty feet high, with a trunk wide enough for someone to hide behind without being seen. Like many old trees, it contained nooks and crannies where animals had dug, the weather had eroded, and the tree grew around itself over time, and Drake, Allie, and Geneva went to work searching while Ingrid stood aside, waiting to jump in if someone wanted to switch out.

"Got it!" Drake said a few minutes later. He was on his knees, clawing at a hole beneath an exposed root. "I can't get it, though. My hands are too big."

"Let me try it," Ingrid said.

She switched places with Drake, and breaking her vow never to put her hand into a hole she hadn't looked into first, she thrust her hand in and immediately touched a smooth metal surface. Ingrid adjusted her hand so she could grip the item, then rotated it back and forth until the tree at last gave up the prize.

"Here it is," Ingrid said, holding up the now-familiar tin box. "All we need to do is go three hours back to Copenhagen and open it."

"No, we don't," Drake said. "I packed the soldering iron, so all we need is an electrical outlet."

Allie took the box and handed it to Drake, then helped Ingrid to her feet.

"Let's go, then," Allie said.

The group moved away from the tree and began the hike back to the car.

"How's the leg?" Geneva asked, taking Drake's hand.

"It's fine," Drake said. "By the time I washed the blood off, it had already stopped bleeding. Won't even leave a scar."

Drake did a double step and yanked Geneva with him until they were walking almost on the heels of Allie and Ingrid.

"I think I spotted your friend," Drake said casually, not breaking stride.

Ingrid exhaled. "I thought that was him. I saw him in Roskilde, too."

"Another lucky coincidence?" Geneva asked.

"I doubt it," Ingrid said.

"What about the other guy?" Drake asked.

"What other guy?" Ingrid said.

"Skinny guy, bald, five-ten, stands perfectly still so we wouldn't notice him. Seems to like a long gray raincoat," Drake said.

Geneva swung her head around. "I don't see anyone like that."

"He slipped back behind the church when we turned this way. I saw him in Roskilde, too."

"You're sure it was the same guy?" Allie asked.

Drake shrugged. "I was a detective for years, you know. I've been out of that game for a while, but I can still spot a tail when I have one."

CHAPTER SIX

The group was within sight of the car when Drake took Geneva's hand and headed for the street. Allie and Ingrid followed behind.

"Hey," Geneva said, surprised by the sudden tug. Rather than break free, she doubled her step to keep up with Drake. "What's the deal?"

Drake pointed at the small building across the street. "Want some ice cream? I could go for some ice cream."

"How do you know they have ice cream?" Geneva asked.

Drake pointed again at the building. "See there?"

The red building had white shutters and white trim around the windows and door, making it appear like 3D representation of Denmark's flag. On one side of the large picture window flew the nation's flag, and on the opposite side flew a flag with an ice cream cone on it. Outside the building were two sets of bistro tables, each with two chairs.

"Grab those," Drake said as they reached the opposite sidewalk. "I'm going to get us some cones. Who wants what? I'm thinking chocolate."

"Chocolate for me, too," Geneva said.

"Strawberry," Ingrid said.

"Mint chocolate chip if they have it. In a dish," Allie said. "Chocolate if they don't."

Drake nodded. "Y'all make yourselves comfortable and enjoy the people watching."

Allie turned and gazed from left to right. "Drake. There are hardly any people… oh. I got you. Yeah. We will." Allie slipped into a seat and invited Ingrid to sit next to her. Geneva grabbed a chair at the other table while Drake entered the shop.

Drake popped out of the building a moment later. He handed cones to Geneva and Ingrid and licked a drop of ice cream from his finger. "Tasty. Anyone have any krone they can spare? I'm a few short and I don't want to charge it."

Ingrid handed Allie her cone, extracted a few bills from her pocket and passed them to Drake before taking her ice cream cone back. Drake stepped into the building and, a couple of minutes later, returned with a cone for himself and a dish for Allie. Before taking his seat, he fished the change out of his pocket and gave it to Ingrid.

"Thanks, Ingrid. I'll pay you back."

Ingrid waved him off. "No need. What's a couple of kroner between friends?"

Drake licked his cone, stood, extracted a wad of napkins from his other pocket, and passed them around. "How's the people watching going?"

Allie circled her spoon inside the dish and took a bite. "This is fantastic ice cream. I think Asger is waiting for us in the parking lot. He's clearly out of his element. I had him in my periphery when you veered off, and he practically jumped out of his skin when he panicked."

Drake smiled. "I know. What about the others?"

"The mysterious man in gray seems familiar with this game. I spotted him on the other side of the church, holding his position. He pops out every so often, pretending to look at the graves. He took off his coat and is clearly keeping tabs on us," Allie said. "Wait a minute, and I'm sure he'll pop up again."

The friends enjoyed their ice cream and two minutes later, a man in a black trench coat emerged from behind the church, sauntered over to a set of graves, and appeared to study them. The way he positioned himself, he could easily keep an eye on the people who were currently keeping an eye on him.

"Is that the same guy?" Ingrid asked.

"Yes," Allie said.

"It's probably a reversible coat," Drake said. "I had one myself at one point. Great for surveillance work when I needed to change my look. It's somewhat effective in a crowd, not so much when you're alone."

As they watched, the man stepped sideways from grave to grave until he reached the end of the row, then went back the way he came and moved out of view behind the church.

"That was fun," Drake said. He had eaten the ice cream below the level of the cone and took a bite.

"What do we do about it?" Geneva asked.

Drake swallowed and shrugged. "There's nothing we can do, unless Ingrid wants to call her new inspector friend. The guy has done nothing except follow us, and always from a distance. We should also consider engaging Asger and try to determine what he's up to."

"I could call him and ask," Ingrid said. "It would be interesting to know why he's been following us."

Drake chomped down the last of his cone and wiped his face and fingers with a napkin. "No. If he thinks we're onto him, he'll try harder to obscure himself. Leave him in plain view where we can spot him. Even if you come face to face, pretend you didn't notice him. We'll find out what he's up to eventually, I'm sure. Should we figure out what's in the box?"

"Where should we do that?" Geneva asked.

"We passed a park on the way in," Ingrid said. "It had a

gazebo. Perhaps it has an outlet," Ingrid said.

"What about Asger and the mysterious man? Won't they follow us there?" Geneva asked.

"I'll drop you three at the park, then keep driving. They'll probably follow me."

"Why don't we go back to our hotel?" Allie asked. "We could do whatever we need to do there."

"What if what we find in the box takes us farther into Denmark?" Ingrid argued. "We'd end up going three hours back to Copenhagen, only to turn around and come back out this way."

Allie thought about it for a second. "But what if we ended up returning to Copenhagen, anyway? There's an equal chance we'd go there."

"True. But we won't know for sure unless we find out what's in the box."

"Okay," Allie conceded. "We swing by the park, but only Drake gets out. That won't take as much time. We'll keep going and circle back around in fifteen or twenty minutes. Will that give you enough time?"

"Plenty," Drake answered.

"Good. We have a plan," Ingrid said.

Not feeling rushed, Allie, Ingrid, and Geneva finished their ice cream while Drake scanned the area for the mysterious man and Asger.

"Y'all finished?" Allie asked. She wiped her mouth, then tucked the napkin into her dish. When the others said yes, Allie collected their used napkins into her paper dish and stepped inside to get rid of the trash.

"Should we do double time?" Allie asked when she returned and found her friends standing and waiting for her.

"I don't think so," Drake said. "We'd look too suspicious. Let's saunter on back to the car, then Ingrid can hit the gas the moment we're out of the parking lot."

Everyone agreed, so they casually strolled to the car like tourists. Ingrid slipped behind the wheel as usual, and Drake got into the front seat.

"How far is the park from here?" Drake asked.

"I don't remember for sure, but it was only a few kilometers," Ingrid said as she pulled out of the parking space, leisurely pulled onto the road, and then pushed the accelerator to the floor. The car jumped forward, pressing all the passengers into their seats.

Ingrid checked her side mirror. "Asger is on our tail."

"Do you think you can lose him?" Allie asked from the backseat.

Ingrid glanced at the speedometer at the same moment they passed a speed limit sign. She did a quick calculation and determined she was already twenty-two kilometers over the limit. Instead of speeding up, she eased up on the gas. "No. I don't want to get pulled over by the police. Or even worse, zip around a corner and run into a bicyclist."

Drake looked in the mirror and saw a car closing the distance between them.

"I have another idea that usually works."

Drake monitored Asger while he explained what he wanted Ingrid to do.

"There's a sign. The park is only a kilometer ahead," Ingrid said. She tightened her grip on the steering wheel.

"Relax, Ingrid, you've got this," Drake said. "Hold on back there." He looked at the speedometer and counted to fifteen in his head. "Park should come up soon."

"It's right around this bend, I think," Ingrid said.

"Okay. Execute the plan."

Ingrid nodded, then removed her foot from the gas pedal. Immediately, the car slowed, and the distance between them and Asger closed quickly.

"Right up there," Drake said, pointing to the side road that led into the park.

"Shh, I'm trying to concentrate," Ingrid said.

Ingrid looked in the mirror. Asger was close enough that she could see a confused look on his face. Her eyes focused back on the road, and she realized she'd almost overshot her target. Ingrid slammed on the brakes and made a sharp turn into the park. Asger, startled by the sudden glare of the brake lights in front of him, hit his own brakes and swerved into the other lane to avoid the collision and flew right by the park entrance.

The roadside park was a small one, with a single road that looped around the perimeter of the park. In the middle stood a small pavilion with a built-in grill standing just outside it, four picnic tables, a one-person restroom, and a water fountain. Ingrid hit the gas again, pebbles from the unpaved road shooting up from her rear tires, and she did a quick loop around the road and stopped long enough for Drake to leave the car. The instant his door clicked shut, Ingrid moved on, and turned left out of the park, heading back in the direction from which they'd come.

The second he was out of the car; Drake ran to the middle of the pavilion and crouched behind a picnic table. He checked the road as he waited, and less than a minute later, Asger drove by the park without so much as a hesitation. The ruse, it seemed, had worked. Drake kept his position for another minute to see if Asger would swing back around and was about to rise when he saw the unknown man pass rapidly by in a dark BMW that matched his sunglasses. He waited another thirty seconds, then stood tall and searched the pavilion for an electrical outlet. When he found one built into a corner support beam of the structure, he removed a thin drawstring backpack from his shoulders and emptied the contents onto the nearest picnic table. He grabbed the soldering iron, plugged it into the outlet, and placed it on its stand. While he waited, he opened a fresh sponge and took the cap off a bottle of water.

Drake sat down, moved the tin box closer to him, and placed

the tip of the soldering iron in a corner of the box. When nothing happened, he put the iron back into the holder and forced himself to count to a hundred and twenty. Holding the box with a towel, he tried again, and this time, the solder beaded and began to flow away from the box. Since it was his second time, he improved his technique and removed the box's cover in under a minute. He unplugged the iron, set it on the stand, and turned his attention to the box. He flipped it upside-down and lifted it straight up. Sitting on the towel was another coin and a tightly folded piece of paper wrapped in plastic. Drake was about to open the paper when he heard a car horn honk. He looked up just in time to see Ingrid race past in the rental. He waited, and less than forty seconds later, Asger drove past, followed by the mysterious man not far behind.

"Time's up," Drake said aloud to no one. He placed the coin and wadded paper back in the tin box and slid the box and its lid into the backpack. He dampened the sponge with the water, then pressed the tip of the soldering iron into the sponge. It smoked and hissed. Drake added more water to the sponge and thrust the iron into it again. Both the smoke and hiss had lessened, and when he did it a third time, there was no reaction at all. Drake licked his fingertips and touched the iron. It felt warm, but no longer hot enough to melt metal, so Drake squeezed the sponge to remove most of the water, then wrapped it around the iron and placed both items into the backpack. He capped the water bottle, added that to the bag, and rounded up the other random items he hadn't used. Drake cinched the backpack closed, then ran to the road. He heard a car coming closer, stepped onto the asphalt, and stuck his thumb out like he was hitching a ride across the country.

Drake's grin left his face when he saw Ingrid speeding toward him. At the last second, she veered to the left and slammed on the brakes. The tires hugged the asphalt, and she stopped close enough that Drake only had to open the door and sit down. He hadn't even closed the door yet when Ingrid sped away; the rental beeping when it realized the passenger had not secured their seatbelt.

"What happened to not wanting to get pulled over for speeding?" Drake asked as he put on his seatbelt. The dinging stopped.

"I'm tired of being chased all over the countryside," Ingrid said.

"There's a roundabout up ahead in two kilometers," Geneva said.

"How many roads?" Ingrid asked.

"Looks like five."

Ingrid pressed the accelerator to the floor, leaving a bit of tire tread on the road and dust swirling in the air behind them. "Five is perfect. Allie, pick a number between one and four."

"One and four? Why?"

"Now, Allie," Ingrid ordered.

"Three?"

"Three it is," Ingrid said. She shifted in her seat and let off the gas only slightly as they passed the sky-blue sign with white arrows that showed they were coming up to a roundabout.

Since there were no other cars entering the traffic circle, Ingrid banked around the circle and turned northward at the third exit. Once through the turn, she punched the gas again and sped forward.

"What's up ahead?" Ingrid asked Geneva.

"There's a small town coming up in about five kilometers."

"Which town?"

Geneva looked at the map. "Givskud?"

Ingrid smiled. "Perfect. We'll go to the zoo."

"Oh, sure," Geneva said as she settled back in her seat.

No one spoke as Ingrid drove. She eased off the gas as she entered the small town, careful not to go over the speed limit, and slowed down even further when they came across a group of cyclists. She followed them for a few hundred meters, then turned down a dirt road and into a parking lot. Directly in front of them was a white building with a red-brown tiled roof. The red letters above the door announced they had arrived at the Givskud zoo. Ingrid shut off the engine and left the car.

"You weren't kidding about the zoo," Geneva said as she left the car and followed her friend to an unoccupied picnic table to the right of the entrance.

"Nope," Ingrid said as she sat. "We probably lost our tails at the roundabout, and if we didn't, we have more than a plausible reason for being here. You know, as tourists."

The four sat around the table.

"Here's what I found," Drake said as he rooted inside the backpack for the items he'd discovered in the box. He grabbed the coin first and put it on the table. "This looks familiar."

Geneva picked up the disc and examined it. On one side was a Viking longship, on the other was a crude spear. She returned it to the table and removed the other two from her pocket and placed them in a line next to the new one. "Looks like a set to me," she said. "I wonder what they are for."

"Then there's this," Drake said, setting the bundled paper on the table in front of Ingrid

Ingrid looked at it for a bit, then picked it up. She grappled with the plastic for a moment, took the Swiss Army knife Allie offered her, and carefully cut away the outer layer. She went to work on the paper, slowly unfolding it, fighting against the stiffness of the paper. When she at last freed the bundle, she smoothed it out as best as she could on the table and discovered she had not one, but two sheets. The first, outer sheet, looked like a crude, homemade wax paper. Turning it over, Ingrid discovered it appeared blank on both sides.

When Ingrid lifted the second sheet, everyone at the table saw it was a remnant torn away from a whole sheet.

"What does it say?" Geneva asked.

Ingrid scanned it for a moment and then began to read. "…and so, my friend, my journey takes me next to see the wicked prince. Perhaps there I will at last receive the details I need to complete this mission. Remember, do it well and do it now. J.L. 2LT."

"That's it?" Drake asked.

Ingrid handed the paper to him, and although he couldn't read Danish, it studied it with interest before handing it back to her.

"So, we're at a dead end," Geneva said, sighing.

"Not quite," Allie said. "If the 2LT after the signature represents a rank, such as second lieutenant, that would help us learn who J.L. is, and maybe that would get us back on track."

"Sure, maybe if he was with the regular army, but what if he was just a part of the resistance movement?" Ingrid said.

Allie shrugged. "I don't know. I think for now we should skip the zoo and find a library or a military museum instead."

Ingrid pulled out her phone and checked the map. "There's not one in this town. The nearest library is in Give, which is about ten kilometers from here. Let's go."

CHAPTER SEVEN

When they arrived at the library, only one computer station was available, so Ingrid brought up an Internet browser, switched it to English from Danish, and Allie and Geneva pulled two chairs in front of the desk to scour the Web for information. Once they got settled, Ingrid disappeared into the library stacks to see if she could dig up anything on the mysterious J.L. in print. Without a computer, and unable to read Danish, Drake wandered outside and sat down on a bench next to the front door.

They worked on their individual efforts for a little over an hour when Ingrid returned with two books in hand.

"Did you find anything?" Ingrid asked.

"We're not sure," Geneva admitted. "Every time we think we're getting somewhere, we run into a Danish website that we can't translate."

"We have a few notes," Allie said, holding up a sheet of paper containing a few dozen lines of scribbles.

"Okay," Ingrid said, pulling up a chair and crowding in next to her friends. "Let's look at what you have first."

"Well," Allie said, "we each had an idea. Mine was to determine if there were any second lieutenants who served in Denmark's army with the initials of J.L." She pointed at her sheet. "There were at least fifteen that we found."

"Okay," Ingrid said. "What was Geneva's idea?"

"She thought we should check if there was any significance to the wicked prince comment in the letter. There were several references we found, both literary and historical, but only one stood out."

Ingrid nodded. "Tell me."

"*The Wicked Prince* was a book by Hans Christian Andersen. He was Danish, wasn't he?"

Ingrid smiled. "He was indeed. Good catch."

"What do you have there?" Geneva asked, pointing at the books Ingrid still held in her arms.

"This is a roster of every man who served in the armed forces during the war," Ingrid said, holding up an aged volume covered in black leather. "Name, rank, unit, where they served, honors received, etcetera. It's in alphabetical order, so you should be able to cross check it to your list." Ingrid handed the tome to Geneva and held up the other book. "This one is even more interesting. It's called *Myths and Missions: The Secret Spies of World War II*. Look here."

Ingrid opened the book and turned it around so Geneva and Allie could see the page. On it was a black-and-white photograph of a smiling man in a military uniform sitting on the front bumper of a truck. He had a wide grin on his face and looked more like he should be picking up a girl for a date rather than heading for war.

"What does it say?" Allie asked.

Ingrid turned the book back around and scanned the pages. "In summary, it tells the story of Jens Lund, who was a second lieutenant in the army. The book says he got discharged for no reason and later joined the Danish resistance movement. He disappeared in 1941. According to the 'myth' part of the story, he was transporting a valuable artifact or information about a valuable artifact. Either way, it was something Hitler was really interested in. It's rumored to be a Viking-era relic that was either stolen by the Nazis during their occupation and Lund stole it back, or Lund had it and the Nazis were out to get it from him. The book is pretty murky on the whole thing."

"So, what happened to him? Or it?" Geneva asked.

Ingrid turned the page and read a little further and shrugged. "I don't know. The author is uncertain whether Lund had it, or if he only knew where to find it."

"Or if the Nazis actually had it," Allie said.

"Right," Ingrid said. "Either way, the story isn't clear at all, and it could be just a local legend."

"What do we do now?" Allie asked. "Go back to Copenhagen?"

"Can I have the letter again?" Ingrid asked.

"Hold on," Geneva said. She rose and left the women. A couple of minutes later, she returned with Drake in tow. "Drake had it," she explained, handing the letter to Ingrid.

Ingrid nodded, took the note, and read it aloud. "…and so, my friend, my journey takes me next to see the wicked prince. To see the wicked prince." Ingrid stopped talking, deep in thought, and no one bothered to interrupt the silence. A few minutes ticked by.

While they waited for Ingrid, Geneva got to work comparing Ingrid's war roster to the notes she had.

"I think," Ingrid said finally, "it may be worth it to visit the Andersen house in Odense."

"Where is that?" Drake asked.

"About an hour and a half from here. But the good news is that it's in the direction of Copenhagen, so we won't be going any farther away from our home base."

"Will we have enough time?" Geneva asked.

Ingrid checked her watch. It was almost three. "Sure. If we keep going and don't dawdle."

"Let's hit the road then," Drake said.

"Hold on," Ingrid said. She took a few moments to take photos of the pages regarding Jens Lund from the myth book and found his information in the other book. and took a snapshot of that as well. She excused herself long enough from her friends to shelve the books and led the party back to the rental car.

Ninety minutes later, Ingrid pulled into a parking garage in the city of Odense, the third largest city in Denmark. They left the car and, guided by a tourist map Allie picked up from an information kiosk outside the garage, they quickly walked five blocks to the Hans Christian Andersen house. They stopped as one outside the building and stared at the entrance.

"This wasn't what I was expecting," Drake said without taking his eyes off of the complex.

"Me neither," Ingrid admitted.

The structure before them wasn't the run-of-the-mill ordinary historic house saved for all posterity. Rather, they stood before a large complex. Close to the door was a map of the grounds, and as one, the group stepped over and stood before it. The display showed not a single house, but rather an entire museum composed of a series of low, round, softly curving pavilions. The pavilions stood adorned in wood and glass, and surrounded them were lavish gardens, maze-like hedges, and lush landscaping.

"This looks new," Drake said.

"As of 2022," Allie said, reading the information from a small plaque dedicated to the architect.

"We're not going to find what we want here," Geneva said.

"Should we go through, anyway?" Allie asked.

Ingrid checked her phone for the time. It was a few minutes until five. She shook her head. "No. It closes soon. This complex is so massive we'd never have time to cover it all today."

"What's the point, anyway?" Allie asked. "They built it eighty years after Lund would have come through here."

"Why don't we go get something to eat?" Drake said. "I could go for a hamburger, or whatever the Danish equivalent is."

"You know, I could eat, too," Geneva added.

"Okay," Ingrid said. She pulled the tourist map from her back pocket and started looking for a nearby restaurant when something else caught her eye. "Can you wait for half an hour? There's one more place I'd like to go first."

"Oh, yeah? Where?" Drake asked.

"To Andersen's other house. Come on."

The friends returned to the parking garage, and within a few minutes had skirted across town and arrived at their new location. Ingrid found street parking, and they clambered out of the car and walked two blocks.

They stood in front of a small, yellow, half-timbered building, a stone's throw from Odense's cathedral. The wooden house looked out of place, surrounded by the concrete structures of more modern times.

"This is open for another hour," Geneva said, noticing the sign on the door. "Should we go in?"

"We might as well. We're already here," Allie said.

They paid the entrance fee and entered the building. Inside, it didn't take long to wander through the three small rooms in which Hans Christian Andersen grew up. Each room emphasized his early years, exhibiting cobbling tools used by his father, and other artifacts related to his childhood and family life. Once they finished inside the house, they stepped into the backyard, where they found a lush garden enclosed by brick walls.

"I see nothing here that's of any help to us," Geneva said.

Allie sighed and put her hands on her hips. She looked one

more time around the small garden and realized Geneva was right. Despite the age of the building behind them, the garden looked recent and well-kept. Even the brick walls had a modern feel about them.

"You're right," Allie said. "We've reached a dead end."

The group left the garden, passed through the home one last time, and found themselves back on the street.

"Maybe whatever we're looking for isn't inside the house at all, but rather somewhere out here." Drake said, motioning to the street and the surrounding environment.

"Take a look around, Drake," Geneva said. "There's nothing here besides this building that looks like it dates back to the war. Everything looks almost brand new in comparison."

Drake scanned the area. Directly across the street was a large four-story red brick building that extended the entire length of the block. Past the corner on which the Christiansen house stood. Drake spotted another modern building that seemed to house apartments. Besides the house, only a two-foot-wide path of cobblestones that ran along the house looked like it had been around for a century. Struck by an idea, he walked to the edge of the property where the cobblestones started, looked down, and scanned each one as he trudged up the street.

"What are you doing?" Geneva asked.

"I'm looking for a long shot," Drake mumbled.

The three women each stepped off the stones and into the street briefly as Drake passed them and followed Drake as he inched his way to the corner. As he turned the corner, something caught his eye. He crouched next to the building, leaned forward, and rubbed a rust-colored cobblestone.

"What is it?" Allie asked.

"There's something scratched into the stone. It says JK41 with an arrow pointing in that direction." Drake raised his hand and pointed down the street of the corner they'd turned. "Think it means anything?"

"The initials of the man, along with the year he disappeared?" Ingrid said. "It can't be a coincidence. I think it means we're going for a walk."

Drake nodded and stood. He kept the lead position, walking down the block, scanning the pavement. The group moved in a single-file line, each paying attention to the ground. When they reached the end of the block, they discovered another rust-colored cobblestone, with the same initials and number, with an arrow pointing to their left. They crossed the street, and for the next forty minutes, moved at a snail's pace, following initials and arrows scratched either into the pavement or in a discreet place on an older building.

"Hold on," Drake said, stopping in the middle of a bridge that traversed a narrow river.

"What is it?" Allie asked.

"I'm out of arrows." Drake pointed to the ground. The pavement appeared fairly modern, made with gray, brown and red bricks, but in the middle of them all was one cobblestone left from a previous era. "This one says 'JL41X'. No more arrows. Does X maybe mark the spot?"

"Under the bridge?" Geneva asked. "Who's going to volunteer to be the troll?"

Allie pointed to the far end, where a paved walking path that ran parallel to the river branched off from the road and headed into a large park. "Let's go over there and see what we can see."

The group moved to the far end, then stepped off the walking path and toward the steep bank of the river. Allie and Geneva sat in the grass, and Drake crouched low.

"This bridge looks fairly modern," Geneva said. "Another dead end?"

"There's a small label on here with the name of the construction company. It says they built it in 2010," Ingrid said.

She moved behind her friends but remained standing. "I'd have to agree with Geneva. It looks like we've hit the end of the road here."

"No. Wait," Drake said. "I think there's something under there." Drake removed his phone from his pocket and took a couple of pictures. He looked at them and expanded the images. "Here. Look." He turned his phone around so the women could examine the photos. "There's an old wood piling here, along with what looks to be some decking."

Allie took the phone from him and manipulated the images. "Okay. It looks like you're right, but that 'X' was in the bridge's center, not on the side. Whatever was there probably got removed when the new bridge got put in."

"I still think it's worth checking out," Drake said.

Without waiting for confirmation from anyone, Drake pushed aside some summer weeds and made his way back to the bridge. Once he could put his hand on the structure, he warily took half a step down the steep bank. As soon as he put weight on his foot, it slid out from under him. He let out a small yelp and pawed at the bridge. His hand found a steel brace, and he grabbed it with both hands and pulled his feet into a position where they were under him again.

"Are you okay?" Geneva asked.

Drake looked back and smiled. She had gotten to her feet and moved closer to him. "I'm fine. Don't come over. It's a lot steeper than it looks."

Geneva stopped and took a step backward.

Drake tiptoed his way down the bank, not letting go of the bridge until he was certain of his footing. He crouched again and checked under the modern deck for a handhold. When he found one, he reached under and grabbed it with his right hand.

Drake saw the new bridge had vertical concrete sides that offered no place to stand, but only a few feet away were the remnants of the original decking, which were a good two feet below the bottom of the current deck.

"Time to make the commitment, Drake," he said under his breath. "Three, two, one…"

On one, he half-jumped, half-swung under the bridge, bending at the waist as he did so he wouldn't hit his head as he went. He flew for a few feet until he felt his feet connect with the deck. It was slippery, and just before he fell, he reached up and grabbed a bridge support from the new deck. Drake shifted his feet until he got his balance, then let go of the bridge and looked around.

"There's another beam that goes across to the other side," Drake yelled.

"Be careful," Geneva hollered back.

There was an eighteen-inch gap between the deck he was standing on and the beam that traversed the river, so Drake reached up again to hold on to the underside of the bridge, then moved his left leg across, then his right. The beam beneath his feet was iron, and only a foot wide. Drake shuffled his way to what he estimated was the center of the bridge, then looked down. A foot in front of him was a wood piling driven into the riverbed. From where he stood, he saw the letters 'JL41X' scratched into the wood like graffiti.

Drake moved his right foot from the beam to the top of the piling, noticing it shift as he did. Quickly, he moved his foot from the piling and reestablished his footing on the beam. Once steadied, he prodded the piling with his foot, noticing that the whole piling didn't move, just the top eight inches of it. Drake crouched, took hold of the beam, then sat, straddling the iron. He pushed himself forward a few feet, then, once the piling was in reach, leaned over and pushed at the wood. He felt something give, then pushed it again. The top tilted. Drake gave it another push, and it came completely loose and dropped into the river below.

"Drake?" Geneva yelled under the bridge.

"I'm still good," Drake called, his words echoing beneath the bridge.

He turned his attention back to the piling and saw a bit of plastic sticking up from the center. He reached over and, with some effort, pulled a tightly wrapped package the size of a half loaf of bread from the wood. Rather than open it, Drake slid the item down the front of his shirt, before reaching into the piling and determining it was now empty.

"And now, to get out of here," Drake said.

Drake sat for a moment, trying to determine the best way to get back to his feet when he realized he couldn't from his current position. Instead, he inched his way backward on the beam until his back contacted the concrete of the new bridge. Using the bridge for support, he clambered to his feet. He stepped to the original deck and reached out for the bridge side.

Drake was trying to determine the best way to get from under the bridge back to the bank when a hand drifted in front of his face.

"Need a hand?" Allie asked from her position on the bridge just above him.

"I don't think you're strong enough to pull me up with one arm," Drake said.

"You're right. I'm not going to. I'll just swing you over to the bank."

Drake considered it for a moment and realized it was either that or jump into the water. "Okay. Take this first."

Drake removed the item from his shirt and passed it to Allie. Her empty hand appeared a few seconds later.

"Let's do this. We're starting to draw a crowd," Allie said.

Drake reached out and Allie clamped her hand around his wrist. She began a countdown. When she got to one, Drake jumped from the deck, and Allie swung him just enough that he headed for the bank instead of the river. Drake landed flat on his stomach, slid a foot down the bank, then stopped when

Geneva and Ingrid each grabbed one of his arms and steadied him.

Once he crawled up the bank and onto the walking path, Drake rolled onto his back and looked up at the faces of his friends.

"I don't want to do that again. I hope it was worth it," Drake said.

Geneva smiled at him, then offered a hand to help him up. "Let's find out, shall we?"

CHAPTER EIGHT

Geneva took Drake's hand and led him away from the riverbank as the four walked along the path. In the distance, Ingrid spotted a park bench, so they adjusted their direction and headed for that. Once seated, Ingrid placed the item in the center of the table and tore the plastic away with her fingers. Once she got through the first layer, the bundle unfolded easily, and before long she freed the item from the plastic and set it in the center of the table.

The wooden box was cube-shaped, each side measuring just under six inches across. Ingrid picked it up and showed the group each side, which featured intricate patterns. Five of the six sides featured geometric designs, and the sixth showed an elephant fending off an attack by hyenas.

Ingrid shook the box, and everyone at the table heard a muted sound from inside. She turned it upside-down, shook it again, but this time no sound came from the box.

"There doesn't seem to be a way to open it," Ingrid said, turning the box over in her hands, looking for a latch.

"Can I see that?" Allie asked.

Ingrid passed the cube to Allie, who studied each side for a few minutes. Allie picked a side and started pushing against different parts of the box, and when she got to the fourth side, a small section of wood slid out an inch.

"It's a puzzle box," Allie said. "There's a way to open it; we simply need to figure out what it is."

"Like what?" Geneva asked.

Allie shrugged. "Depends on who made it. It could be a series of sliding panels, like this one I moved, or rotating rings, kind of like a Rubik's Cube. We won't know for sure what it will take to open it until we do it."

"Why don't we simply break it open?" Drake asked.

Allie smiled. "Always wanting to bash something, aren't you? We could, but we don't know what's in it. There might be something breakable in there, and we wouldn't want to destroy whatever's inside."

Drake shrugged. "I guess not. I was simply making a suggestion."

Allie turned the box over several times. "Sometimes the maker will leave clues to the solution, such as in the patterns, colors, or textures on the box."

"But we won't know that until we open it?" Ingrid asked.

Allie smiled. "Now y'all are catching on."

Allie brought the box close to her eyes and studied it carefully. When she spotted no visual clues, she slowly ran her fingertips gently along all six sides of the box searching for any seams, imperfections, or giveaways that might lead to the secret of opening the item. Finding nothing, she let out a heavy sigh and began attempting to move random tiles on the box.

Drake watched her for several minutes, then let out a long, loud, audible sigh that lasted for a good fifteen seconds. "How long is this going to take?" he asked.

Allie set the box on the table in front of her, crossed her arms, and gave him the stare-down. "Well, it will take from the time I start opening it until the time we find out what's inside. This thing might open in six moves, or it could open in a hundred. We won't know until we know."

Drake shoved his hands in his pockets and moved to sit.

"Hey, Drake," Geneva said, "why don't we go for a little walk? I need to stretch my legs."

"I don't feel like it," Drake responded, almost in a huff.

Geneva rolled her eyes, grabbed Drake by the shirtsleeve and pulled him to his feet. "Come on, grumpy-pants. Let's see if we can find something to drink. I'm quite parched. We'll be back in a bit," Geneva said, turning her attention to Allie and Ingrid.

The women sat at the table and watched as Geneva took Drake's hand and led him down the path farther into the park. They moved at a slow, somewhat steady pace, less like they were on a mission to find refreshments and more like they were two young lovers moving through the park. They watched as Geneva pointed out something in the distance, and the couple stopped to watch for a moment before they began their stroll again.

"I've seen her do that before," Ingrid said. "I suspect we won't see them for about an hour."

"Seen her do what?" Allie asked as she picked up the box and examined it again.

"Get into slowdown mode. She's done that to me a few times. Usually when we've been out on longer geocaching days and she's tired, or when we're out shopping and she wants to stretch out the experience a little more. Suddenly she becomes interested in everything, whether it be a puffy cloud, or a really tall tree, or a rock with an interesting shape. Once she stopped in front of a storefront in some small town we passed through and awed at a dress color she claimed she'd never seen before."

Allie raised an eyebrow. "Was it unique?"

"Pink, Allie. It was pink. What woman has never seen a pink dress before? She just stopped in front of that window so she could have a chance to rest and slow things down for a moment."

"Why doesn't she simply say that? When I'm tired and need

a break, I'll say so. We're not out here on some race or something."

Ingrid shrugged. "I don't know. I think she has a fear of disappointing people. Allie, I do hope she was serious about finding drinks, though. I could certainly use one."

Allie smiled. "Me too."

Allie went back to work on the box, holding it firm with her fingers while trying to slide different parts of the parquet pattern with her thumbs. After a few moments of manipulation, Ingrid cheered when a half-inch piece of wood slid away from the box.

"Well done!" Ingrid exclaimed.

Allie grinned and looked up at her friend. "Save some of that cheer. We've still got a long way to go with this thing."

Allie focused on the areas of the box adjacent to the piece of wood she'd moved, and when that didn't yield any results, she rotated the cube and worked on the side around the corner from the wood. After a few seconds, a second tile shifted, and she pushed it out with her thumb. Once again, she attempted to move the tiles around the one she'd just moved with no luck. Allie rotated the box a quarter-turn, and it wasn't long before a third piece shifted. She put the box down, cracked her knuckles, and smiled.

"I think I'm onto something," Allie said as she shook out her hands.

"What?" Ingrid asked.

"Once I find a piece, I need to rotate the box counterclockwise and go from there. Let's see if I'm right."

Allie retrieved the box, pointed out to Ingrid the last piece she moved and turned the box to the fourth side. It took only a minute before another piece slid away. With four pieces opened, Allie positioned her hands on the top and bottom of the box, and gave it a shake, expecting it to open and reveal whatever was inside. The box didn't budge.

"Shoot," Allie said. "There must be more to this than I'd

hoped. Hold on."

Allie turned the box to the first piece she'd opened and worked all the possibilities with no luck. She repositioned the box, so she was facing the top, worked her magic, and a minute later a fifth tile slid aside. She rotated the box and soon got into a rhythm. After twenty minutes, over two dozen pieces of wood had slid away from the main box and pointed in every direction like a porcupine that had run through the spin cycle on a dryer. She rotated the box and worked at the few remaining tiles that hadn't moved. None of them did. Allie pulled on the first section she'd released, and to her surprise, the entire section came away from the box. She looked into the void and saw a button the size of a pen tip.

"Do you have a pen on you?" Allie asked.

"Of course. I'm a geocacher," Ingrid said. Ingrid retrieved a pen from the backpack she wore and handed it to Allie.

"Thanks," Allie said. She took the pen, lined it up with the button, and pushed.

A quick click resonated in the air, and Allie smiled and sat back.

"I think that did the trick," Allie said. She handed the pen back to Ingrid and cracked her knuckles again.

"Open it!" Ingrid yelled, her excitement brimming.

"Nah, let's wait for the others," Allie said.

"They've been gone forever. Who knows when they'll return?"

Allie pointed to a spot over Ingrid's shoulder. "I estimate they'll be here in three minutes or less."

Ingrid pivoted and saw her friends heading toward her. "Drake's carrying a bag. I hope they brought the drinks."

"You seem better," Allie said as Drake threw his leg over a seat and situated himself at the picnic table. "Not so crabby anymore?"

Drake smiled. "I'm good. I think my blood sugar was low.

Geneva made me eat a chocolate bar and a cola, and I'm doing much better now." He turned to Geneva, who had taken the seat next to him, and patted her on the knee.

"Did you bring anything back for us?" Ingrid asked.

"Oh, yeah." Drake opened the bag. "We got orange and grape sodas, chips, and chocolate for everyone." He spread the bounty onto the table, and each person selected the items they were interested in and began the impromptu picnic.

Allie polished off a bag of sea salt and vinegar potato chips before emptying a bottle of orange soda. She wiped her fingers on her pants and gestured at the box.

"I think it's ready to open," she said. "I heard it click a minute before y'all got here."

"What are you waiting for?" Geneva asked just before she took the last bite of a chocolate bar, rolled up the wrapper, and dropped it into the empty plastic bag.

"We were waiting for you to get back," Ingrid said. "Now that you are, let's do this."

Allie nodded and picked up the box, careful not to move any of the pieces she'd slid out. She gripped the bottom firmly, then pulled on the top. She expected some resistance, but it slid apart easily, revealing a section inside the box the size of two decks of playing cards stacked atop one another.

"Do it," Allie said, setting the box on the table in front of Geneva.

Geneva peered over the box, then took from it a package wrapped in plastic and secured with twine. After she undid the twine, she slipped a fingernail under the plastic and slowly pulled. It separated, and she unfolded it fully, revealing a piece of parchment. When she picked up the paper, she tilted it slightly and out dropped another coin. It hit the table, bounced once and appeared to be headed for the ground when Drake snatched it out of midair.

"It's another coin," Drake said, turning it in his fingers to look at both sides.

"Is it like the others?" Ingrid asked.

Drake looked at the obverse. "The longship is the same. This one has a trident on the back." He examined the coin a moment longer, then set it in the empty box. "What else do you have there?"

Geneva unfolded the parchment to its full size, which was roughly ten by ten, had it been complete, but there was a part that someone had torn away, making a rough arc in the page, as if a shark had bitten it.

"Is that a map?" Allie asked.

The image on the paper looked crudely drawn. One continuous line traced from the top corner of the page and ended where the sheet had torn, but it appeared to be a coastline, as outside the line were a half-dozen rough circles that appeared to be islands, and a group of flowing triangles that seemed to represent water. Inside the lines were four squares and nine triangles. A thin line joined them like a necklace, then trailed off the page that was missing.

"Looks like one to me," Ingrid said.

"Is it of Denmark?" Drake asked.

Ingrid shrugged. "No clue. I suppose I could compare it to Google Maps and see if it lines up with anything. Or… Hold on. I have a better idea." Ingrid pulled out her phone, took a few minutes to search for some information, then placed a phone call. Several minutes of conversation passed before she finished the call. "Okay, we're all set. I've made an appointment with a history professor at the university, which is only a few blocks from here."

"What does this say?" Geneva asked, pointing at the map.

Ingrid noticed Geneva had flipped the parchment over and there was writing in the lower corner in modern Danish. She struggled to read the script but finally got it.

"It says don't trust anyone," Ingrid said, looking up from the page into the eyes of her friend.

"We need to go," Drake said. He grabbed the box pieces without asking Allie to close them and dumped them into the plastic sack. "Our friend in the gray coat is back. He hasn't spotted us yet, but I'm sure it won't take long. Ingrid, you take the map and head for the university, and the rest of us will split up. We'll meet back at the car in an hour."

"Wait, are you sure it's the same guy?" Geneva asked.

"Allie?" Drake asked.

Allie turned around, so she faced the path they'd walked down to reach the picnic table. She put her hand above her eyes to shield the sun, then watched a man in a gray coat take a phone from his pocket and look at something on the screen. He then appeared to dial a number, placed it next to his ear, and turned so he faced the park. The man spotted Allie and started walking toward the group.

"It's him. Let's do what Drake said. Meet back at the car."

Ingrid quickly refolded the map, then shoved it into the back pocket of her jeans, stood, and hustled away, following the paved path to the north.

As Geneva rose, Drake handed her the bag.

"Keep the coins safe," he said. "Go that way." Drake pointed toward a path that cut west, went over a small footbridge that spanned the river and continued back into the town.

Drake and Allie watched as Geneva half-walked, half-jogged down the path.

"You go that way," Drake said, pointing to the east. There wasn't a paved path in that direction, but there was a dirt trail where park patrons had worn a rut in the grass as a shortcut to the far side of the lawn.

"Which direction are you headed?" Allie asked.

"South," Drake said.

Allie nodded and started walking, turning her head so she could keep an eye on the stranger, who had picked up his speed.

She noticed his head was moving back and forth, as if trying to decide which of the four people to follow. He seemed to make a choice, then changed his direction and headed toward Geneva, who was just approaching the bridge. The man began to jog and made it a dozen steps before Drake came out of nowhere and slammed into the man, sending them both to the ground. In an instant, Drake was on all fours, crawling away while trying to get to his feet. The man reached out, caught Drake's left foot, and held firm. Drake brought his knee back as much as possible, then kicked forward, driving his foot through the man's grip and connecting with his chin. The man's head snapped back, and he released Drake. Drake crab-walked back a few feet, then flipped over, found his feet, and ran away.

Allie kept moving but monitored the man. He stayed on the ground for a few seconds, rubbing his chin. The man attempted to pull himself from the ground, caught his foot on his trench coat, and fell. Allie giggled, then grew serious again when the man made it to his feet and glared in her direction. He spun to look for Drake, who had since vanished from sight, then turned back to Allie and made a beeline for her.

Allie turned forward and picked up her pace into a light jog. At one time in her life, she considered herself an excellent runner. She'd run on the track team in high school, and when she joined the service, she'd been one of the fastest people in her unit, often beating out most of the men in footraces, but injuries and getting older had both taken their toll, and it wasn't long before she felt a hitch in her side and needed to slow from a jog to a brisk walk.

Allie turned and made a quick glance around. She saw none of her friends, which was good, and determined the stranger had halved the distance between them, which was bad. Allie pressed forward and came to the end of the park. Still moving, she scanned the area to determine the best direction to take. To her right were a row of apartment buildings; to her left, a block down, was an open-air market. Any easy decision, Allie broke to the left, jaywalked across the street, and headed for the market.

Allie looked behind her, saw he was only a hundred yards away, and despite the pain in her side, picked up the pace again until she got to the market. She moved in among the booths of people selling everything from fresh vegetables to homemade candles to small, crocheted animals. Allie looked in vain for a side alley, a door to slip through, or any other passage that would lead her away from the area, but she found none.

The stitch in her side doubled in intensity, causing her to stop in her tracks. She grabbed a canopy leg, and bent over, breathing deep and hoping the spasm would pass so she could keep moving.

Someone spoke to her, and she looked up at a white-haired woman who sold vegetables at the booth Allie had stopped at.

Allie shook her head. "I'm sorry. I don't speak Danish."

"Are you okay?" the woman asked, switching to English.

Allie pointed behind her. "There's a man after me." Allie raised her head to see if she could spot him, but didn't.

The woman nodded. "Bad breakup?"

"I wish," Allie said.

"Come here," the woman said.

Allie stood and entered the booth. The woman took off her green windbreaker and, while Allie put it on, the woman produced a baseball cap featuring the name of her farm and slipped it onto Allie's head.

"Sit," the woman said, pointing to a short wooden stool. When Allie sat, the woman shoved a small crate of tomatoes into Allie's lap. "Head down, look for imperfections."

Allie did what she was told and started inspecting tomatoes for problems. She spotted a wormhole in one and set it aside. Allie remained dedicated to the task, and five minutes later, from the corner of her eye, she spotted the man in the gray coat stop at the booth. She could feel him scrutinizing her.

The white-haired woman said something in Danish to the

man. He grunted in return and left the booth.

"I assume that was him. Nasty looking man. You keep looking through those tomatoes, and I'll let you know when he's gone."

Allie gave a nod and breathed easier.

CHAPTER NINE

Ingrid sprinted out of the park and after two blocks settled into a comfortable jog until she recognized the comfortable rhythm of her shoes slapping the pavement at regular intervals. She hadn't run in a while, but she had always enjoyed it enough that she had done a handful of marathons. She had to cut back to half-marathons and 5k's, but that wasn't because she didn't love to run, just that she didn't always have the time to commit to the training schedule that she did when she was at her peak. Ingrid crossed the street, ran a block, had to wait for a light to change, and ran another block. Confident that the man chasing her would have caught her by now, she slowed from a jog to a fast walk to a saunter before spotting a bench at a bus stop. She pulled the phone from her pocket as she sat down and brought up the map.

"Damn," she muttered when she realized she'd run away with no real thought to where she was going and ran several blocks in the wrong direction. Ingrid checked the time, realized she needed to hustle, and went back into run mode.

Up ahead, she spotted a group of tourists waiting for a bus, so she stepped into the bike lane as she ran past them, checking the street sign to ensure she headed in the right direction. Ingrid didn't notice that the light had changed, and she heard a horn blaring as she darted into traffic. She turned in time to see the Volkswagen bearing down on her, then watched as the front end dipped as the driver slammed on the brakes. Instinctively, she dropped her hands to the car's hood, as if she could push the vehicle away.

"I'm sorry," Ingrid stated in Danish as she held up a hand in apology.

She pivoted to return to the sidewalk when she heard someone calling her name.

"Asger?" she exclaimed when she recognized the driver, now standing near the front bumper. "What are you doing here?"

Asger hesitated, then stammered. "I'm here on an errand for the museum. What are you doing running in the street? Where are your friends?"

It was Ingrid's turn to hesitate. In her mind, the seconds it took to compose an answer bled over into minutes and then hours. "Back at the hotel. We're visiting the region. They wanted to rest, and I wanted to go for a run."

"Okay," Asger said.

Ingrid could tell by his furrowed brow and skeptical gaze that he didn't believe her. She didn't care.

"I don't want to hold you up. We'll be back in Copenhagen later in the week. We should get together for drinks or dinner." She forced a smile. "Thanks for not running me over."

Rather than wait for a reply of any kind, Ingrid checked traffic, crossed the street and resumed her run. As she jogged, she turned her head to catch the reflection in the plate-glass windows of the shops she passed and noticed that Asger was following her. She slowed to a stroll, hoping that it would persuade him to pass her, and instead he pulled to the curb and idled while she walked. Ingrid checked her map and noticed the college campus began one block over, so when she reached the corner, she turned and walked on the side street until the road ended at a parking lot. When she got past the first section of cars, she began to run, navigating through rows of vehicles, and once she hit the large green space that made up the college quad, she bolted as fast as she could. Unexpectedly, she turned right, entered the science building, and wandered around until she found a side door to exit. Ingrid stopped, and when she spotted no one but students milling about, she checked her map, caught her bearings, and headed for the humanities building.

Ingrid used the directory to determine which room held the professor's office, then climbed the stairs to the third floor. At the end of the hallway, she knocked on the ajar door and stepped in.

She expected a history professor's office to be nothing but bookshelves and dusty tomes, with a large oak desk piled high with papers to grade, but the office she entered contained a modest, modern desk adorned with a lamp and a laptop, with two chairs in front of it and a blond woman who looked to be in her early twenties sitting behind it, busily tapping at the keys.

"I'm here to see Professor Olesen," Ingrid said.

The woman looked up, then stood. "I'm Professor Margrethe Olesen. You can call me Marg," the woman said, extending her hand.

Ingrid shook hands with the woman but stayed in an awkward silence.

"I've heard it before. I look too young to be a professor," Marg said, gesturing to a visitor's chair while she took her own. She redid the hair tie that kept her shoulder-length hair out of her face, then smiled warmly at Ingrid, her blue eyes twinkling. "I'm actually twenty-nine. I have my parents and both sides of my family to thank for good genes."

Ingrid sat in silence, shifting in her chair.

Marg smiled again. "You said something about a map?"

"Oh, yes," Ingrid said, snapping back into the moment. She pulled the square of parchment from her pocket, leaned across the desk and handed it to Marg. "It's probably not even real, and I apologize in advance for wasting your time if it isn't, but I wanted to get it checked out."

Marg took the item, felt its texture and dropped it on the desk. She opened a drawer, extracted a pair of nitrile gloves and donned them. She moved her laptop to the floor, then unfolded the document and spread it out flat on her desk.

"I can tell by feel alone this is authentic parchment, most likely goat or sheepskin. I'd have to have it analyzed to get more specifics on that."

"What about the writing?" Ingrid asked. "Is it a map? If so, can you tell what it's of?"

Marg studied the lines on the document. "It appears to be. Let's go find out for sure."

Marg refolded the map and stood. Ingrid followed her into the corridor and waited while Marg locked her office. Together, they walked down the hall to the stairs, then descended into the basement. They stopped outside of a locked door, but with a wave of Marg's key card, the door clicked open, and as they stepped into the room, the lights came on.

"What is this place?" Ingrid asked, looking around.

The walls were white; the overhead lights were LED. In the center of the room stood a large table that looked like an X-ray machine. Along one wall was a large display screen with four computer stations directly beneath it. Off to the side stood a bank of industrial-sized printers, along with a common office copier.

"We call it the Mapper 3000," Marg said. "I'm proud to say that we have only one in Scandinavia, and to be honest, I'm surprised it's not in use."

"What does it do?"

"Watch and try to contain your amazement!"

Marg unfolded the map, set it on the table, and attached clamps on all four sides to keep it in place. Once the task was complete, she moved over to the computers, opened a program, and selected several parameters. She hit a green button, then leaned back into a chair and folded her arms.

"You might want to sit down. This may take a while."

The machine above the map hummed, then moved from side to side, not unlike the scanner in Ingrid's home printer.

"What's happening?" Ingrid asked.

"It's taking a scan of the image," Marg said. "Look at the screen."

Ingrid turned around and looked at the wall monitor. Slowly, the map image transferred from the page to the computer.

"How is making a copy going to help?" Ingrid asked.

"Patience. The magic hasn't happened yet."

Ingrid sat back and watched.

"Where did you find this, anyway?" Marg asked. "You didn't steal it from a museum, did you?"

"It's a long story."

"We've got some time," Marg said.

Ingrid hesitated, wondering what to tell the professor. It was an unlikely and unbelievable story, but in the end, she decided on the entire tale, leaving out the part about her suspecting her friend Asger of following her all over the country. When Ingrid finished the story, Marg opened her mouth to speak but got interrupted by a series of loud beeps.

"What's happening?" Ingrid asked.

Marg grinned as she pointed at the screen. "This is when the magic starts."

Ingrid looked up and saw the lines of her map turn into thick black lines. A moment later, a series of red lines overlaid the black lines. They didn't match exactly, but part of it did, so that line stayed and the rest flickered and changed positions.

"What's happening?"

"The computer scanned your map and is now comparing it to every other map in the database."

"For all of Denmark?" Ingrid asked.

"Sure. It will start with Denmark, since that's what I programmed it to do, but if we don't find a match there, it will move on to other locations along the Baltic and North seas and will keep going until it finds as close of a match as it can."

"How can it do that? It's hand-drawn and could be from anywhere. And who knows what the scale is. Those little triangles could be across the street, or countries apart from each other."

Marg shook her head. "I don't know all the mathematics involved, but I know it works. It considers things like scales, populations, landmarks. Like I said. It's magic."

The women sat for a moment watching as red lines filled in. The incorrect lines disappeared and got replaced with other options. At the same time, the computer replaced the triangles on the original map with rough circles. The machine beeped three times in quick succession, then returned to its starting position.

"Ah," Marg said. "Well, I can tell you your map is authentic and old."

"How can you tell?" Ingrid looked at the screen, where most of the black lines had red lines superimposed on them.

"Give me a second," Marg said. She turned her attention to the computer, selected a few more options from the program, and updated the screen. As Ingrid looked on, labels appeared on the screen. A few contained names; the others only numbers, and a few remained unlabeled.

"What you have here is a map that, although I can't date it precisely, goes back to sometime around the ninth century." Marg produced a laser pointer and shined a green dot on the screen. "These numbered locations, which appeared as triangles, depict Viking settlements in the Jutland region, most of which we uncovered over the decades. As you see, there are three on your map that we can't account for. I'd bet my bottom krone that we'd find remnants of Vikings there if we looked. Would you mind if

I kept a copy of this?"

Ingrid nodded. "Sure."

"Thank you. So, you have a starting location over here…" Marg pointed to a large city on the coast, "that runs from settlement to settlement until it goes over to the part of the map that we don't have."

"Can the computer extrapolate it?" Ingrid asked.

Marg frowned and shook her head. "No. If there were only a quarter or less of the map missing, we might be able to do it, but there's too much missing. The computer could make its best guesses, but the margin of error would be too high to trust."

"I understand," Ingrid said. "So essentially, this is what? A trade route?"

"Oh no. Whatever this goes to wouldn't be that trite. If this dates to the ninth century, it would have been incredibly expensive and time-consuming to even produce this parchment, so someone wouldn't have used it for something as mundane as remembering a trade route. Whatever this leads to was something important."

"Like what?" Ingrid asked.

Marg leaned back in her chair again. "I've studied hundreds of sources of Viking legends, and among the most widely told involve a Viking hoard, where they stored the combined riches of several Viking leaders."

"Like a central bank?" Ingrid asked.

Marg nodded. "Something like that. Although the Vikings created settlements and weren't nearly as nomadic as typically depicted in stories and films, they still had to deal with invaders, traders, explorers, and others. They felt that, for the sake of the community, it was best to keep their treasures in a central location, rather than lose them if a hostile force blew through the town. Granted, that's what the legends say."

"What happened to the horde?"

"No one ever found it, so far as I know. The Viking age lasted for over two hundred years, and although the legend of the horde has survived, it's doubtful that the horde did. My best guess was that as the Vikings got assimilated into other cultures, the horde got divided up and distributed among the leaders."

"And you think my map might lead to the horde?" Ingrid asked.

"Only a possibility. It could also lead to someone's grandmother's house, or to a neighboring country or city. It's hard to tell without the other half of the map."

"Where would I start?" Ingrid asked. "If I assumed that the treasure existed."

Marg glanced at the monitor for a while and then shined the pointer on the city from where all the directional lines started. "Aarhus. You know it? Up on the Jutland Peninsula?"

Ingrid nodded. "My parents are from Jutland. Any ideas where?"

Marg shook her head. "I don't know. The city itself started in the latter half of the eighth century. If I were going, I would find anything dating back to that era. It's possible that nothing still stands, though."

"I think something might," Ingrid said.

"Why?"

Ingrid moved to the map, undid the clamps holding it down, flipped it over, and pointed to the message on the reverse side.

"Don't trust anyone," Marg said, reading the message.

"That message doesn't date back to the ninth century."

"I agree." Marg picked up the map and tilted it to scrutinize the message. "Based on the ink and the script they wrote it in, I'd say it's modern, anywhere from the 1930s to the 1950s."

Marg folded the map and passed it to Ingrid. "If this does go to the horde, you'd better be careful. This message implies other people know about it, and treasure hunters will go to any extremes to find what they're searching for, even in this day and age. I'm going to download your data to a hard drive that I'll keep in my possession for the time being, and when you've exhausted your search, let me know and I'll bring the rest of this map to light to determine if there really are other settlements to explore."

"Thank you," Ingrid said. She slid the map back into her pocket.

Marg returned to the computer, pushed a couple of buttons, and one of the printers roared to life. She retrieved the sheet from the machine and handed it to Ingrid, who saw it was a hard copy of the screen display.

"Good luck on your quest. And be careful," Marg said.

"Of the other treasure hunters?" Ingrid asked.

"Yes. And the curse, of course."

* * *

Ingrid waited inside the door of the humanities building and looked around for Asger. She didn't see him anywhere, so she slid through the door and slowly descended the steps. At ground level, she spun around again and saw no one except a bunch of girls who clustered in a group while walking across the quad. Ingrid waited until the posse got near, then joined them.

"Hello," a brunette said as Ingrid got into the correct cadence to merge with the group. "Nice day for a walk, isn't it? I've never seen you before. Are you going to the science building? That's where we're going."

Ingrid stammered. "Science. Yes. I'm new here. I'm going to the science building."

The brunette said nothing else as the group plodded on like a school of fish to the far side of the campus.

Ingrid joined them as they entered the building, then continued down the main corridor and straight out the back door of the building, which opened into a small parking lot. She looked around for Asger's Volkswagen, but didn't see it. She opened the map on her phone, determined where she was and where she'd left the rental car, then began walking.

Ingrid noticed the time and realized she was over forty minutes late. Checking her messages, she saw there were more than a dozen she hadn't read, along with as many calls she had missed from Allie, Geneva, and Drake. She sighed, prepared her apology, punched in Allie's number, and made the call.

CHAPTER TEN

"How long have you been awake?" Allie asked, propping herself on her elbow. There was just enough pre-dawn light coming through the crack between the hotel room curtains to see Ingrid was sitting at the desk.

"An hour or so. Did I wake you?"

"No. What's going on?"

"Not much. I've been up for a while, thinking about this whole thing. This was supposed to be a fun, relaxing vacation. Geocaching, visiting some places that are near and dear to my heart, but here we are, going all over the country chasing clues to, what, a horde of treasure that probably doesn't exist?"

"I don't know. I reckon it is kind of fun. Like geocaching on a grander level," Allie said. "We've done this before. What's really bothering you?"

Ingrid's silence filled the dark room.

"Is it your friend, Asger, showing up at the wrong place and wrong time? Or the mysterious man in gray?" Allie asked.

"Don't forget about the police inspector," Ingrid said.

"Ah, yes. Inspector Lisa?"

"Louisa," Ingrid said, holding up a business card she dropped on the desk. "If we were just chasing down leads, that's one thing, but why in the world would three different people be interested in what we're doing?"

Allie got up, plodded across the room, and wrapped her arms around Ingrid's shoulders. "Maybe it's because there's something to the legend, and somehow we've gotten closer to it than anyone else ever has."

"But it was an accident. If Geneva hadn't stumbled upon that first box…"

"Doesn't matter. We're here now. What do you want to do? Stop the search? Go back to the intended itinerary? Return to America, defeated and broken?"

Ingrid giggled. "Defeated and broken?"

Allie shrugged. "Seemed apropos."

"What do Geneva and Drake think?" Ingrid asked.

"I don't know. We haven't talked about it. Why don't we discuss it at breakfast?"

Ingrid activated her phone. "That's three hours from now."

Allie squeezed her girlfriend a little tighter. "Good. Come back to bed. I'm cold."

* * *

"…so, what do you think?" Ingrid said. She'd spent the previous ten minutes telling her friends her thoughts while enjoying breakfast.

"Well, to be honest, the pace has been a little hectic to me," Geneva said. "It seems like we get into these situations and rush around to the point where I can't even catch my breath."

Drake nodded as he broke off a piece of the blueberry bagel he'd been devouring. "I kind of agree with Geneva. Also, I've been looking forward to taking the bridge to Marmot and getting a cache in Finland."

Ingrid's head tilted as she processed his statement for a moment. "I assume you meant Malmö. And it's in Sweden."

Drake shrugged while he chewed. He took a moment to swallow, then downed half a glass of orange juice. "You got the idea. It would be fun to get a cache and a souvenir from another country."

Geneva nodded in agreement. "I could get on board with that."

"Allie? What is your opinion?" Ingrid asked.

Allie sipped her cup of cinnamon tea, then placed it on the table before her. "It sounds like we could use a break from all the adventure. Where did you say the next town is?"

"Aarhus? It's three hours from here if we take the ferry, and add another half hour if we drive the entire way."

"And Sweden?"

"An hour or more, depending on traffic and how efficient the border patrol is."

Allie had more tea. "Why don't we take a day? Go find a geocache or two in Sweden. Tomorrow we can pick up the quest. Or if we're still feeling burned out, the next day. Or next week. If there is a secret treasure and it's still out there after a thousand years, another few days of not being found won't hurt it."

Ingrid remained silent for almost a full minute, then nodded. "Okay, it's settled then. After breakfast, we all grab our passports and head to Sweden. Unless there are any objections."

The group had none, and they returned to small talk as everyone finished eating. After breakfast, they gathered their geocaching gear and headed to the car. Allie, Geneva, and Drake marveled at going over the scenic Oresund bridge while Ingrid easily navigated a four-mile tunnel that extended from Denmark to an artificial island in the middle of the strait before it transitioned into a five-mile bridge that showed off the spectacular views as they moved closer to the Swedish coast. It took only a few minutes to get past border control, and once in

Malmö, Ingrid pulled into a parking lot and waited for directions while Geneva and Drake found nearby geocaches to search for.

"Ingrid, do you know Swedish?" Drake asked.

"A little. What do you need?"

Drake read as best as he could the description of the cache they'd selected.

Ingrid smiled, then laughed. "I'm not sure if the words you just said make sense in any language. Let me see what you have."

Drake passed Ingrid his phone. She took it and read. "This cache is a magnetic nano located near the park's entrance. Available during daylight hours early. Bring your own pen."

"I understood you only knew a little Swedish. That was impressive," Geneva said.

Ingrid handed the phone back to Drake. "It isn't that impressive. Swedish and Danish are closely related languages. It's the dialects that usually trip me up when hearing it. Reading it is much easier, both for Danes reading Swedish and for Swedes reading Danish. Where do we need to go?"

Drake checked his phone. "The park is four blocks that way," he said, pointing to the right.

Ingrid put it in gear and within a few minutes she parked in a designated space just outside the park entrance.

The park itself was surrounded by a four-foot-high wall made of bricks and stones. At the entrance stood an iron gate with a plaque that included the park's name and hours.

"Near the park's entrance. If it's a magnetic nano, it must be on the gate, right?" Geneva said.

"Makes sense to me," Allie said as she stepped over to the gate. Rather than running her fingers over the rust-flecked gate half covered in spiderwebs, Allie stepped through the gate and closed it behind her. She scanned the gate, looking for anything that seemed like it didn't belong. On the other side, Geneva and Drake did the same from their perspective, while Ingrid checked out the braces that attached the gate to the wall.

"Got it," Ingrid said. She used the tip of her pinkie finger to coax the half-inch nano from its hiding spot in a small depression where the brick met the brace. She unscrewed the container and unrolled a log that was barely the size of a fingertip. Ingrid wrote her name on the log, then passed it to her friends before putting it all back together and placing it back exactly where she'd found it.

"There's another cache in this park," Drake said, handing the phone to Ingrid.

"No need to disturb the flowers or the ground cover. Stay on the paths. Look chest high," Ingrid read before returning the phone.

Drake looked at the compass and pointed into the park. "That way. Follow me."

The group followed a pebble-covered path farther into the park, which transformed from green space into a botanical garden. The path took them past a small rose garden, featuring several varieties and colors of roses, then they passed through a section of colorful perennials and annuals, a section popular with dozens of fat honeybees moving from flower to flower in the early-morning sun. A hundred yards later, the path moved into a small bunch of trees. Each group of trees they passed differed from the previous one, and each variety included a small sign giving the tree the scientific and common names.

"We're almost there," Drake said, leading the group another fifty feet up the trail.

"Quercus robur, the English oak," Ingrid said, reading the tag near the trunk of the mighty tree. It towered a good thirty feet above the group and had a trunk five feet in diameter.

"Big tree," Drake said.

"They get much larger," Ingrid said. "This one is a baby in comparison."

"Where do you suppose the cache is?" Geneva said.

Drake studied the tree. It contained no obvious holes. "The

hider must have attached it to the bark somehow."

Drake began to step to the side of the tree when Ingrid grabbed his arm and held him back. "No. The description said to stay on the path."

Drake moved in front of the tree and began running his hand along the rough bark. "If it's here, it's well camouflaged." He seemed methodical in examining the tree, moving his hand from waist to head height along the rough bark before adjusting his hand to the right and repeating the process while his friends looked on. When he reached the middle of the tree, he stopped and grinned. From under a loose piece of bark, Drake pulled a small pouch, wrapped in camouflage tape that matched the color and texture of the bark. After everyone signed the log, Drake took care to replace it.

"Let's head back to the car," Ingrid said. "There are a lot of virtual caches I'd love to do in the city center area."

The group followed the path headed to the main gate, and had gotten as far as the edge of the trees when Drake stopped.

"What?" Geneva asked.

"Shh. Look at that man over there."

The group peered into the park, and wandering through the garden was a man who looked somewhat familiar.

"That can't be him, can it?" Allie whispered.

"It certainly can be," Drake said. "I got a really close look at him yesterday, and I think he's the same guy who's been following us."

Allie peered into the distance and watched the man as he turned down a path that moved away from them. "Yeah, I guess you're right. I wonder what he's doing here."

"I doubt he's here to smell the flowers. We need to leave," Geneva said.

"Agreed," Allie said. "Let's go that way." Allie pointed to a path that branched off to the right instead of the left. "If he gets close. We'll separate like we did yesterday and meet back at the car."

The friends hastened their steps and rushed along the path. Eventually, it reached a point where it would curve back around and head toward the main gate.

"Stop," Drake said. "Let's jump the fence here. That way we won't get boxed in if he's waiting for us at the entrance."

"Good idea," Ingrid said.

Drake left the path and pushed his way between two lilac bushes, holding the branches ahead of him so they wouldn't snap back on Geneva, who was right behind him. Five feet later, he came to the wall, leaned over, and saw they had come out around the corner from where Ingrid parked the car.

"The coast is clear," Drake said. He put his back against the wall, crouched, and interlaced his fingers. "You first, Geneva. I'll help you over."

Geneva put her foot into Drake's hands, and Drake lifted her. She sat on the wall, swung her legs over and dropped to the ground on the other side.

"I'm over," Geneva said.

Ingrid and Allie joined her within a few seconds. Drake was last, having to pull himself onto the wall before hitting the earth next to his friends.

"Let's get out of here," Drake said.

They turned the corner, saw the rental waiting for them, and ran to it. Ingrid got into the driver's seat, turned on the ignition, and put the car into gear before the other three doors closed. As she pulled away from the curb, the man rushed out of the park and into the street, followed by another man.

"He's got a friend," Ingrid said, watching them rush to a car of their own through the rearview mirror.

"Where should we go?" Ingrid asked.

"Head toward downtown. Hopefully, we can find either a lot of people or a police station," Allie answered.

Ingrid drove, following Allie's directions as she navigated

using her map.

"Are they following us?" Drake asked.

Ingrid checked her mirror. "I don't think so."

"Go in there!" Allie said.

Ingrid looked forward in time to make the turn into a parking garage. She entered, and Allie directed her to find a spot on the third of four levels. Ingrid did, backed into a stall along a wall, and killed the engine.

"Drake, do you know what I think?" Allie said.

"That this guy must be tracking this car? I've been having the same thoughts."

Drake and Allie got out of the car. Although sunlight peered in from the structure's side, they each turned on the flashlight on their phones in order to get enough light. They each took a side of the car and began checking for a transmitter. Methodically, they began at the back bumper and worked forward, checking the back wheel well, then under the car, moving forward inch by inch.

"I've got it," Drake said as he pulled himself out from under the car, just behind the front tire.

Allie joined Drake at the front of the car, and he handed the tracker to her. It was a small black box, about the size of a matchbox. On one side, a red light blinked, showing it was active.

"Should we destroy it?" Allie asked.

Drake shook his head. Rather than disable the unit, he turned around and placed it on the wheel well of the gold Toyota parked in the spot next to them.

"Keep checking. We'll make sure there's not a second one on the car," Drake said.

The pair returned to inspecting the car. While Allie checked the trunk, Drake checked the engine. Neither found anything else out of the ordinary. They took their seats, and Ingrid pulled out of the stall, crept through the parking garage, and exited.

Several hours later, Ingrid parked a new rental car in the

hotel parking lot.

"That was a fun time," Allie said. "I'm glad we managed to shake those guys and salvage the rest of the day. It was a good idea to go up the road to Lund."

Ingrid smiled as she grabbed her pack from the car. "Why should our day get ruined just because we're being pursued by strange men? Besides, since you and Drake are confident you got the tracker, I didn't think we'd have any other problems with them."

"Not today, anyway," Allie said.

Allie and Ingrid said goodbye to their friends at the hotel's main entrance. Drake and Geneva headed to their room while Allie and Ingrid carried on to theirs.

"Good idea changing rental cars," Ingrid said.

Allie laughed. "I saw it in a spy movie once."

Allie took her keycard, unlocked the door, and entered the room. Inside was pure chaos. An intruder threw the bedding on the floor; the mattress was ajar. Picture frames looked crooked, every drawer pulled out, clothing scattered everywhere.

"Aw, crap." Allie rushed in and went right to the desk. She looked around and removed the blanket partially draped over the desk chair and looked under the desk. "They got the puzzle box."

"Oh, no! Did they get the map?" Ingrid asked.

"I hope not," Allie said. She made her way to the curtains, pulled them back, and checked the bottom hem. From Inside a small pocket, where Ingrid had snipped a few of the stitches, Allie pulled out the map, and the printout Ingrid had gotten from the university. Allie exhaled. "We're good. We should see if anything else is missing."

The women were picking through the room and checking their possessions when there was a knock at the door.

Ingrid answered, and Geneva and Drake entered.

"Oh, no. You got hit, too," Geneva said as her eyes settled on the mess.

"They stole the puzzle box," Allie said. "I loved that thing. Great construction. Did they take anything from you?"

"All the clues and tin boxes. We had them all in one bag, and the entire bag was missing," Geneva said. "The only thing they missed was the coins."

"They weren't in the bag?" Ingrid asked.

"No. I had them on the desk in a plastic cup from the bathroom. Drake's been putting coins in the cup that he's collected along the way. The cup was untouched."

"That's good," Allie said.

Ingrid frowned. "What do we do now?"
"First, I think we need to contact the front desk and report the break-ins. Otherwise, I think we're fine if we want to continue the quest. Everything taken was a clue to something we've already found. We still have the map and the knowledge that we need to head to Aarhus next." Allie said. "That is, if we want to keep going."

No one spoke for a minute.

"Well, I'm interested. I'd like to see this thing through," Drake said.

"Even if we find nothing at the end, I'm having fun exploring Ingrid's homeland," Geneva added.

"Ingrid?" Allie asked. "What do you think?"

"I'm really not ready to go back to Boston yet," Ingrid answered.

"It's settled then," Allie said. "Tomorrow, we head to Aarhus. That leaves only one more thing to talk about."

"What's that?" Drake asked.

"Who's going to make my bed?" Allie said, pointing to the messy room.

CHAPTER ELEVEN

The trip across the Great Belt strait took roughly ninety minutes. Rather than drive the entire way, the group decided to take the ninety-minute ferry ride to save miles, time, and energy. Each person handled the cruise in their own way. Allie read a paperback book she brought with her, Ingrid played games on her phone, Geneva passed the time by people watching, and Drake slept. The wind blew in from the north, making the early-morning temperatures seem that much cooler, forcing everyone to wear either a sweatshirt or a jacket. As the ferry made its way across the water, seabirds followed, searching for food kicked up by the propellers.

"Do you know where we should start when we get to Aarhus?" Allie asked Ingrid, peeking over the top of her cozy mystery.

"There's an Old Town Museum. My plan is to go there, check if there are any structures or sites that go back to the forties or earlier. I'm not sure how much of the town got affected by the war," Ingrid said, putting her phone on the seat next to her. She yawned, then stretched her arms high over her head, interlocked her fingers, and shifted in her seat.

"It's way too early," Ingrid said. "I could have used another hour of sleep."

"Hour? I could have used six," Allie said.

"How long should we keep this up?" Ingrid asked. "To be honest, I'm getting tired, and would love to slow down for a bit. Perhaps we could visit a museum, or have a picnic in the park, or do something else like regular tourists would do."

Allie gave her a tender smile. "Those sound like great ideas. Why don't we take a day off tomorrow?"

"You know, Aarhus isn't that far away from the town my parents are from."

"Perfect. We should go there today then. You could show us around, and we could have lunch."

"I could eat," Drake said. He appeared to be sleeping, with his jacket covering his chest, and his eyes closed.

"Of course you could," Geneva said.

Allie was about to add her own comment when an announcement over the ship's speakers declared they would arrive soon and those with cars should return to them and prepare for docking. The friends rose, took the stairs down to the car deck, and got into their vehicle.

In all, it took twenty minutes to leave the ferry after it touched land, and another fifteen to drive to the Old Town area. Ingrid parked in front of the information center and turned off the engine. From her seat, she could read the open hours on the building's door and checked her phone.

"We're early by an hour," Ingrid said.

"Good. We can get some breakfast," Drake grumbled from the back seat.

"Stay here," Allie said.

Allie left the car, moved to the building's entrance, and from a display case retrieved a brochure and map of the area. She studied it for a few moments before returning to the car.

"I think we have a problem," Allie said. "Although the buildings around here are from as early as the mid-1500s, they got moved here from other parts of Denmark and aren't the oldest structures in the city."

"What is?" Geneva asked.

Ingrid got on her phone to find the answer. "Aarhus Cathedral. Parts of it date back as far as 1201, and it expanded between 1450 and 1520."

"Is it still standing?" Allie asked.

"Yep," Ingrid said. "And it's only about five minutes from here." Ingrid started the engine and pulled out onto the street.

"Before we go to church, can we find some food?" Drake asked.

"Excellent idea, Drake," Ingrid said. She brought up the map on her phone, fidgeted with the buttons for a moment, and changed course to head to the nearest open restaurant.

The friends arrived at the church door twenty minutes early and waited patiently for it to open, and when it did, a tour guide greeted them, an older man dressed in black slacks, a white shirt, and a red vest. He wore his white hair parted on the side and combed over the top of his tortoiseshell glasses.

"Welcome to Aarhus Cathedral," he said in Danish.

Ingrid moved to the front of the group, shook the man's hand and told him she was the only one of the four who spoke the language.

"Deutsch"? The man asked.

Ingrid shook her head. "English."

"Ah, I should have known." The man grinned and opened the door wider to allow everyone entry. "Based on the accent, I'm guessing America?"

"Yes," Ingrid said.

"Well, I will start over then. Welcome to Aarhus Cathedral. My name is Peter. I'd be happy to give you a guided tour, or you can wander around by yourselves. You'll find a lot to explore here. We have the largest collection of frescoes in Denmark, the largest stained-glass window in Denmark, an altarpiece made in 1479 that has movable panels that change with the liturgical seasons, and an oak-carved pulpit from 1588. Of course, we also have our famous votive ship, and a pipe organ made in 1730. Both are also the largest in Denmark. Of course, there are also many chapels, tombs, and memorials spread throughout the cathedral. Is anyone interested in a tour?"

"I am," Geneva said, raising her hand like a schoolgirl offering an answer to a question.

Peter smiled. "Great. Anyone else?"

"He will too," Geneva said, grabbing Drake's hand before he had a chance to respond.

"Excellent," Peter said. "Anyone wanting the tour, follow me and we'll get started."

Peter led Geneva and Drake farther into the cathedral, leaving Allie and Ingrid on the doorstep.

"What should we go check out?" Ingrid asked. "The organ? Perhaps some of the tombs?"

"I don't know," Allie said. "Let's wander around and see what we can."

The women walked deeper into the cathedral, both awed by the expanse of the largest and tallest church in the country, as well as the architecture of the five-hundred-year-old building.

"This place is huge," Ingrid said as they stopped in front of yet another fresco, this one depicting St. Christopher and St. Clement. "If we find anything in here, it will be a miracle."

Allie eyed the fresco. She glanced for a moment at St. Christopher, who stood in the foreground holding a sword, but it was St. Clement who really grabbed her attention. St. Clement was in the background, with a staff in one hand and an inverted anchor in the other. Beneath the anchor was a small circle, and within that circle was a boat.

"Does that look familiar?" Allie asked, pointing at the spot on the fresco.

Ingrid scrutinized it for a moment. "It kind of looks like the boat on the coins Geneva found."

"It does indeed," Allie said.

Allie took a picture of the fresco and expanded it to examine it more closely. A thin brown line exited the coin and ran in a series of curves that appeared to make up the robes of the saint, and eventually the line ended at another circle.

"Look at this," Allie said, pointing to her phone.

"It's a sunrise," Ingrid said. "Like the coin,"

"That's what I thought, too."

"The line goes through it. Where to?" Ingrid asked.

"I don't know. Maybe we need to find another fresco," Allie said.

The pair wandered through the cathedral until they found the fresco of St. George slaying a dragon. Within the art, they found another circle containing a boat with a thin brown line that led to a circle, this one containing a small snake. Knowing they were on to something, Allie and Ingrid moved through the cathedral with a purpose, scrutinizing every fresco they came to. By the time they finished a loop around the cathedral, they had located only two frescoes containing circles.

"It sure would be nice if the frescoes were all in one place," Ingrid remarked. "I'm sure we missed something."

"We have them in a book."

Ingrid and Allie turned around to see Peter approaching them with Geneva and Drake behind him.

"Book?" Allie asked.

"Sure. From our gift shop. We have many books dedicated to the cathedral, including one that spotlights all the amazing frescoes we have."

"Where is it?" Allie asked.

Peter pointed toward the door they'd entered. Had the group turned left instead of right when entering the cathedral, they would have run right into it.

"Thank you," Allie said, already headed in the direction he suggested.

"And thanks for the tour. It was amazing," Geneva said, following her friends toward the shop.

Once inside the tiny store, it didn't take long for Allie to find the book section, and after a quick scan of the covers, she selected a book with a sampling of frescoes on the front. She paged through it until she got to the photo of St. George, saw what she hoped she would, and moved to the photo of St. Clement. She nodded when she noticed the same circles and lines she had on her phone. Allie checked the first pages of the book and learned it had come out only a few short months before. She took the book to the counter, paid for it, and left the shop.

Allie thumbed through the pages as she waited outside for her friends to appear.

"Do you think we can find some tracing paper?" Allie asked when Ingrid joined her.

"Tracing paper?" Ingrid repeated as she thought. She dug her phone out of her pocket and did a quick search. "I don't see any stores in the area where we could get that. Would parchment paper work? There's a grocery only a few blocks from here."

"I think it would," Allie said.

Twenty minutes later, the friends clustered around a table inside a small restaurant within the shadow of the cathedral's tall steeple. Allie hunched over the book, looking for more clues. She had already traced the lines from the St. Clement and St. George frescoes onto parchment paper using a black Sharpie. She'd found a third circle, this one containing a spear, inside the fresco featuring St. Michael weighing souls on the day of judgment. Allie, wanting to be thorough, returned to the book's beginning and started leafing through the pages a third time, inspecting every inch of each fresco within.

"These look the same," Geneva said, staring at the three

sheets of parchment paper on the table.

While Allie looked up from the book, Geneva took the three sheets and placed them on top of each other, then held them up to the light. Although the lines diverged in a few places, they always realigned farther along in the drawings.

"Here's your strawberry pie, sir," the waitress said, trying to get Drake's attention, who had been watching Geneva line up the papers.

Drake glanced at the waitress, then shifted his arm to make room for the plate. "Thank you," he said. He looked at the pie, smiled, and picked up a fork.

"Are you interested in the limestone mines?" the waitress asked.

"Limestone mines?" Allie asked.

The waitress smiled. "Yes, of course. They've been pulling limestone out of the mines for centuries. My grandfather used to work at one. He had tunnel maps just like that," she said, pointing to the papers in Geneva's hand.

"Can I get you anything else?" the waitress asked.

"Yes. More information on the limestone mines," Ingrid said, laughing.

The waitress shook her head and left the table.

"What are the odds that these random lines are actually part of some mine?" Drake said. He glanced at the tip of the pie on his fork, then slipped it into his mouth. He chewed for a moment, then grinned. Drake set down his fork. "That is the most delicious pie I've ever had."

"Pretty slim, I'd guess," Allie said, remarking on his mine comment and ignoring the pie.

"I think that too," Ingrid said. "Did you guys see anything else in the church while you were on your tour?"

As Drake worked on the pie, Geneva answered the question. "No. I don't think so. I think we were pretty thorough, too. While I slowed us down and asked questions, Drake looked at everything as closely as he could."

Allie drained her glass of water and then carefully set the glass on the wet ring it made on the paper napkin beneath it. "Okay. Then this is probably a dead end unless we can figure out what the lines mean."

Drake licked the remaining morsel from his fork and pushed his plate aside. "Well, maybe we can still salvage this day and find a few geocaches before we head back to Copenhagen."

Ingrid nodded in agreement.

Allie looked at her friends. She gave a curt nod, then waved to get the attention of their waitress.

"Can I help you?"

"Can I have the check, please?" Allie asked.

"Of course. How do you intend to pay?"

"With a card."

"I'll be right back."

The waitress left the table, leaving the friends alone.

"There seems to be a handful of caches in town," Drake said. "This multi-cache is only a mile from here."

"Is it a long one?" Geneva asked.

"I don't know," Drake said. He handed his phone to Ingrid, who read the description and told the party it was a five-stage cache that would take them all over Aarhus.

"Got anything easier?" Geneva asked as Ingrid gave him his phone back.

As Drake searched for an appropriate geocache, Allie folded the papers and tucked them into the book. She turned her head in time to see the waitress approaching, so she dug into her wallet and pulled out a credit card.

The waitress showed Allie the bill, and Allie nodded, then inserted her card into the handheld card reader the waitress had. Allie finished the transaction and waited for the receipt to be printed.

"Thank you," Allie said.

"Thank you," the waitress said as she gathered up Drake's plate and silverware. She left the table and headed toward the kitchen.

As she put her card away, she dropped a few kroner on the table for a tip.

"You know that's unnecessary," Ingrid said, pointing at the coins on the table.

"I know. Not tipping is a hard habit to break. Is it okay to leave this, though? She won't find it insulting or anything?" Ingrid eyed the coins, then picked up about half and handed them back to Allie. "What you have there is sufficient. You've already paid a service charge."

Allie accepted the coins and slipped them into her pocket. As a group, they rose and headed for the door. They were out on the street already when the waitress rushed from the restaurant, caught up with them, shoved a pamphlet into Ingrid's hand and disappeared into the diner without saying a word.

Ingrid stopped and looked at the paper. It was a tourist brochure for a defunct limestone mine not far from town.

"Anyone up for a trip underground?" Ingrid asked, holding up the paper for all to see.

"Sure!" Geneva and Drake said almost simultaneously.

"No way," Allie grumbled.

Ingrid took Allie by the arm, leading her to the car. "You can stay above ground. We won't force you to go with us into the hole."

They piled into the car and made it to the quarry within thirty minutes. As they entered the inky blue visitors center, Ingrid approached the ticket counter to inquire about tours while her three friends wandered about the rest of the center, which included a tiny gift shop and a large display of the area's history.

"Look at this," Geneva said, getting Allie's attention.

Allie wandered to Geneva's side and glanced up at the wall display that had captured Geneva's attention.

Before them there was a map of the limestone mines, complete with air shafts, tunnels, dead ends, and elevators.

"Do any of these match the drawing we have?" Geneva asked.

"I'm not sure," Allie said. "And I think it would be a little obvious if we held up a tracing to the wall and tried to find a match."

"Agreed," Geneva said. "Why don't you give me one of your copies, and I'll keep an eye out for anything when we go below."

"Good idea." Allie retrieved the book from her pack and took out one tracing and handed it to Geneva. "I'll keep poking around topside and see if there's anything to see. I just hope we've got the right place."

Geneva reached out, putting her hand on Allie's shoulder. "Keep up with the positive thoughts. If we're on the right track and find something, that's great. If not, the three of us get an adventure for the day."

"What do I get?" Allie asked.

Geneva thought about it for a few seconds. "Well, you get to stay up here. And you get to have a little peace and quiet away from the rest of us for an hour or so."

Allie smiled. "I do get the best part of the deal."

"Hey, we've got to catch the tour," Ingrid said, interrupting the conversation.

They said goodbyes, and Allie watched as Geneva, Ingrid, and Drake clustered into a small group with a half dozen other people. Everyone on the tour received a hardhat to wear, and as the guide began giving out a safety briefing, Allie did a quick lap around the information center, left the building, and found a bench on the far side of the building. She sat in the shade and began to wait for her friends to return. After a few minutes, she grew bored, so she extracted the frescoes book from her pack and started it from the beginning. The first few times she'd gone through the book, it was in the context of searching for clues, but this time, she started at the first page and read through it like any other casual read.

Allie heard a car come into the parking lot, and on instinct she looked up. At first, nothing seemed awry, but as soon as she spotted the strange man who had been tailing them, a chill ran down her spine.

CHAPTER TWELVE

"How deep does this go?" Drake asked the tour guide.

The tour guide, used to Danish, began to answer in his native language before his brain realized he needed to switch to English. "Not far. Only one hundred meters."

"That's just over the length of a football field," Ingrid whispered to Drake.

Drake rolled his eyes. "Thanks, but I already knew that."

As the group descended farther into the limestone mine, the guide gave a brief history of the mine, which dated back several centuries, starting with the earliest Viking settlement in the area. With every few meters, the temperature dropped, which was the reason the guide recommended each person on the tour carry a sweatshirt or jacket with them into the mine.

While the guide droned on, the group paid rapt attention, listening to details and snippets of information. Eventually, the elevator stopped with a jolt. The doors shook open, and the guide stepped out and to the side and ushered everyone out of the elevator.

He stepped over to a rusty mine cart loaded with rocks. On

top, there were a variety of tools, from a worn pickax to a candle-lit miner's hat. As he picked up each item and explained its purpose, Geneva pushed herself to the rear of the group and pulled her map from her pocket. She looked at it intently, trying to memorize it in case she didn't have a chance to refer to it while on the tour. She'd been so involved with the paper, she didn't notice Drake leaning over her shoulder, seemingly doing the same thing.

"What should we look for?" Drake asked.

"I'm praying for a map hanging somewhere on these walls that looks just like this one with marks showing both our current location and where the treasure is," Geneva said.

Drake gently kissed the side of her neck. "That's probably unlikely, dear. But perhaps we'll find some offshoot veins or paths, or whatever they call them in the mining world."

Ahead of them, the crowd moved forward, the guide at the front, with Ingrid, Geneva, and Drake bringing up the rear.

LED lights strung along the walls near the ceiling lit the space nicely, ensuring top visibility as they strolled through the mine, with the guide providing almost unending discussion about the place, including the amount of limestone produced through the years, the means of extraction over centuries, and the occasional lime pun that didn't hit right, since they were based more on the fruit than the stone. The guide had upped the pace from a light saunter in the beginning to an almost frantic gait, as if he needed to catch a train. They moved so fast, they almost walked right past an ancient wooden door.

Geneva skidded to a stop and pointed at the door. "Excuse me. What's this?"

The guide turned around, stopping so suddenly that the man behind him bumped right into the guide, causing the guide to shift. The man mumbled an apology and sheepishly took a sudden interest in his shoes.

"I'm sorry?" the guide asked.

"Where does this go?" Geneva asked, pointing at the door.

The guide waved her off. "Nowhere. It was a passage to another part of the mine, but a cave-in several decades ago made the route impassable. Now, please if you'll follow me."

The guide turned, and the group followed as the ground sloped down.

"I'd love to check behind that door," Geneva said.

"I bet you would," Drake answered. "There are probably a thousand tunnels, shafts, and passages in here. There's no way we'd be able to inspect each one."

"I don't doubt that. But since that's the only one we've seen since we've been down here, that's the one I want to inspect."

The ground sloped more, and two hundred yards later, it leveled off, and they came to the edge of a large underground lake.

"All aboard the boat, please," the guide said.

Geneva hesitated for a second and took a step backward. "No!" she yelled for all to hear.

* * *

Allie sat still, watching as the stranger and his friend walked from car to car, peering in the windows. She had the idea they were trying to figure out which one she and her friends now had, ready to drop another tracker behind the bumper, she assumed. As she pretended to read a book, she used all her brainpower to keep the men away from the rental, and when they approached, they gave it a cursory glance before moving on.

Allie picked her cell from her pocket, brought up Ingrid's number, and made the call. It rang a half-dozen times before Ingrid's voicemail picked up. She tried again, and after she got the same result, she tried Geneva's number. Allie didn't bother listening to Geneva's entire message before ending the call. Since Drake wasn't a believer in voicemail, his number rang a dozen times before Allie gave up and put her phone away. She slid off the bench and slowly walked to the building, trying to appear as natural as she could. As she entered, she saw the two men speaking to the ticket agent. Allie got close enough to overhear the conversation, but since it was being held in Danish, she backed off to the far wall and pretended to study a display. From where she stood, she watched the men in her periphery as the ticket agent pointed at a clock above the counter, then at the elevator behind her that led to the mine. When the men made a move for the elevator, the agent protested, but when the second man produced something from inside his coat and showed it to the agent, he calmed down and let the two men pass. The stranger pressed the call button, and everyone stayed motionless while waiting for the elevator car to appear.

* * *

Exasperated by the delay, the tour guide stepped through the crowd to where Geneva stood.

"What is the problem?"

"I'm not going on that thing!" Geneva screeched, pointing at the boat waiting to take passengers across the lake.

"But the tour goes this way. Surely you were told about the boat when you bought the tickets."

"I didn't buy them. She did," Geneva said, pointing at Ingrid.

The tour guide looked at Ingrid, whose cheeks reddened. She shrugged.

"The tour continues on the other side of the lake. If you come to the boat, we can move on. I can assure you it is very safe. Besides, the lake is only a few feet deep at its worst. You'll be fine."

Geneva pointed again and stepped toward the guide. "I. Don't. Go. On. Boats," she said, punctuating each word from her mouth.

Behind the guide, the others on the tour began to get restless.

Drake stepped up, put his arm around the guide's shoulder, and led him a few feet away from Geneva.

"You'll have to excuse her," Drake whispered. "When she was little, she was out fishing with her father and the boat overturned. Her twin sister and she both fell into the water. Her father could only reach one, and her sister died. She carries a tremendous amount of survivor's guilt."

The guide looked Drake in the eyes, his face softening. "Is this true?"

Drake nodded. "It is. She gets this way every time we go near a boat of any size. I apologize."

"I understand now. If she goes back the way we came, she can go to the elevator and ride it up to where the tour began."

"I'll go with her to make sure she's okay."

"Tell the agent upstairs to refund your money and please give your friend my deepest apologies."

"Thank you," Drake said. He removed his arm and returned to Geneva, taking her hand. "It's okay. You don't have to go on the boat. I'll take you back. Ingrid, why don't you enjoy the rest of the tour? We'll meet you upstairs."

Ingrid nodded.

"Okay, everyone. Onto the boat. We're behind schedule," the tour guide said.

"Keep a lookout for anything that looks promising," Geneva whispered to Ingrid.

"I will. Be careful." Ingrid turned, walked to the dock, and climbed aboard the small boat. The tour guide nodded to the boatman, a small engine started, and the vessel began a slow journey across the water.

"Come on," Geneva said, pulling at Drake's hand. "Let's go take a peek at the passage."

Within a few minutes, they returned to the door. Although

there was a large keyhole, Drake pulled on the latch, and it opened freely. A cloud of dust exited and slowly settled on the floor.

"That was lucky," Drake said.

"For sure."

Geneva entered the passage first. They'd made it in only a few feet when it got dark enough that they needed to rely on the flashlights on their phones to see by. Unlike the main tunnel, this one was dark, much colder, and not as easy to traverse with rock debris that littered the trail.

They'd made it only a hundred feet when Geneva shuddered, turned, and focused her light on Drake. "Maybe this wasn't such a good idea. Do you think we should go back?"

Drake hesitated for a moment, considering his reply. "Why don't you stay here, and I'll go up the tunnel just a little farther and see if there's anything to see? That guy said the tunnel got blocked anyway, so chances are we'll be turning back."

"Okay. Go. But be quick about it, okay? I don't like being here. I can see now why Allie doesn't enjoy going underground."

"She developed that phobia during active combat, so at least there's no one shooting at us."

Geneva's chin moved, turning her attention to something moving in the tunnel. "Did you catch that?"

Drake focused his attention. "No. What was it?"

"Nothing, hopefully. Go. Explore, but do it quickly. Don't forget to come back for me," Geneva said.

Drake kissed his beloved on the forehead. "I'll be back before you know I'm missing."

Geneva watched as the light on Drake's phone grew fainter, and after a few moments disappeared altogether.

* * *

"Carl, I can't believe you dragged me down here," Elias said, an edge on his voice.

"I'm paying you well, so I'll drag you wherever I need to. And I told you. No names."

"Who cares? Who is going to notice in this dank place what your name is?"

Carl turned on a dime, grabbed his partner by the shoulders and pushed him hard enough against the wall for Elias to lose his breath.

"You have two options," Carl whispered.

Elias tried to back away, but the earthen wall prevented him from moving. He could feel Carl's hot breath in his ear.

"You can do what you're paid to do, which is take my orders without question, or, if you prefer, you can have an accident sometime today. And trust me, your family, if you have any, will have great difficulty identifying your body afterwards. Now. Make a choice."

"I'll… do what you say," Elias stuttered.

"Everything. No more second chances. Got it?"

Elias nodded. Carl held him for a second longer, then released him and backed away a few steps.

"Come on. We need to see if we can catch up with them."

Carl started a light jog along the tunnel, with Elias right on his heels. A few minutes later, they arrived at the underground lake, with no boat in sight.

"Now what?" Elias asked.

Carl peered across the water, then at his associate. "We passed a door. Let's check that."

The two turned around and trudged up the tunnel. When they came to the door, Carl opened it and gazed into the darkness.

"Now what?" Elias repeated.

"Now you stop asking me that question," Carl said. "It's getting on my last nerve. Why don't you try being quiet for a while?"

Elias took the hint, gave a single curt nod, and stepped backward.

Carl retrieved his phone, turned on the flashlight, and almost immediately saw two sets of fresh footprints in the settled dust. "Before you say it, yes, it might not be them, but unless you want to go for a swim, I suggest we see where these lead."

Carl stepped into the tunnel. Elias followed. They'd traveled only a few hundred feet when Elias stepped on a rock and turned his ankle. He yelped, staggered, and was about to fall when Carl grabbed his arm and steadied him.

"Quiet," Carl warned as Elias' echo died in the tunnel.

* * *

"What's up, buttercup?" Ingrid asked as she joined Allie beside the wall display.

Allie, so focused on the elevator, didn't notice Ingrid's approach and jumped, startled, before she turned around and saw her friend standing there.

"Where did you come from?" Allie asked.

"I finished the tour. It ended at a different elevator in that green building about two hundred yards north of here," Ingrid said.

"Where are Geneva and Drake?" Allie asked.

Ingrid moved closer and lowered her voice. "We spotted a side tunnel. The tour continued on a boat across an underground lake. Geneva pretended to have a fit to avoid the boat. The tour guide sent her back to the beginning of the tour, but I suspect she really wanted to check out that tunnel. I assume they haven't come back up yet?"

"No. And we have another problem. That strange guy and his friend, who have been following us, showed up. They just went down in the elevator."

"Crap," Ingrid said. "How did they even know we were

here?"

"I didn't stop them to ask," Allie said.

"The tour is a one-way loop, so if Geneva and Drake haven't come up, they either headed through the tunnel they found or continued on in the direction of the tour."

"Or they've gotten caught," Allie said.

"Let's hope not. We'll go to the tour exit and wait for them there. Hopefully, they'll be up soon."

Ingrid and Allie moved swiftly toward the exit and stepped out into the afternoon sun. Ingrid took only a few strides before she halted.

"Hello, Ingrid. I've finally found you." Asger grinned.

***

Geneva, hearing what sounded like an injured animal behind her, focused her light forward and took a few tentative steps following Drake's footprints. She thought her sharp ears had caught something and picked up her pace to a fast walk. She stepped on a rock, stumbled forward, but righted herself and kept moving. Twenty yards later, she came to where the ceiling had caved in. She stopped, wondering if she'd passed a side tunnel. Geneva focused her light on the ground and spotted Drake's footprints. They led to the far wall, and there she spotted a hole through the wall the size of an easy chair. Based on the fresh marks in the dirt, Drake had crawled through.

Geneva bent over and leaned into the hole. "Drake? Can you hear me?"

Geneva didn't get a response, but a second later, she noticed a light coming in her direction. After a few moments, Drake appeared.

"I thought you were waiting for me," Drake said.

"I heard something. Drake, I think we have company," Geneva said.

"Tour guides?"

"I don't think so."

"Come on," Drake said, holding out his hand.

Geneva took his arm, and Drake helped her through the hole.

"There's a branch in the tunnel up here," Drake said. "I didn't know which way to go, so I was headed back to you."

Drake escorted Geneva another seventy yards through the tunnel and stopped where it forked off into two possibilities.

"Which way?" Drake asked.

Geneva moved from one tunnel to the other, shining her light on each. "I don't know. It's a coin flip."

Geneva pulled the map from her pocket and studied it for a moment. "Do you think we came any of these ways?" Geneva asked, holding out the map.

Drake glanced at it and shook his head. "You've got me. It could have been any of these. Or none of them."

"I was afraid you were going to say that," Geneva said. "Let's go this way."

Geneva moved into the tunnel on her left and followed it as it curved to the right, then back to the left, as if they were following a serpent's back. They'd traveled a quarter mile when Geneva suddenly stopped. She moved backward, as if her subconscious directed her to reverse, then shined her light on the wall.

"Look at this," she said.

As Drake joined her, Geneva pointed to a circle the size of a cookie. Etched inside the shape was a small boat with what looked to be an arrow pointed down. She dropped the light, focusing it on the space a few inches above the floor.

Drake got on his hands and knees and ran his fingertips along the wall. "This feels different, and there's a color variance, too." Drake rapped on the stone and then on the wall next to it. "I think it's hollow."

Drake got to his feet, got into position, and kicked at the wall. He flinched, half expecting to stub his toes, but his foot broke right through the wall. He went to his knees, shined his light into the hole, and extracted a small wooden box.

"Does this look familiar?" he asked, passing the box to Geneva while he got to his feet.

They both turned when they heard voices in the tunnel behind them.

Geneva shoved the box back into Drake's hands. "Let's keep going."

They moved as one through the tunnel. They came to a branch, then in short order, another. Rather than asking which way to go, Drake followed Geneva's lead as she guided them through. At last, their luck ran out as they came to an enormous pile of boulders.

"Dead end," Geneva said, turning around. "Maybe we should take another tunnel."

"No, wait," Drake said. "Look. There's light."

Geneva eyed the small button of sunlight streaming in from the outside. "Can we get through there?" she asked.

"Hold this stuff," Drake said, passing his phone and the box to Geneva. As she trained the light on the wall, Drake pulled at a few rocks the size of basketballs. Eventually one tipped, and rolled to the floor, landing just in front of Geneva's feet. He moved a second, then a third rock. Drake stepped on a boulder that lifted him fifteen inches higher, then turned around, putting his back to the next rock. He pushed upward, straining his muscles. Geneva watched as his cheeks reddened and his body shook. Drake rested for a moment, then gave the boulder a second heave. A cracking sound shot out, and suddenly Geneva saw open sky.

Drake scampered up through the hole, then leaned back in, offering his hand. Geneva passed him his phone and the box, then accepted his hand.

"Help me with this," Drake said, pointing at the small boulder he'd dislodged. Together, they pushed it over the hole they'd crawled through, then Drake added a few more rocks to the top, blocking the hole as best as he could.

"Where do you suppose we are?" Drake asked, brushing his hands together to remove the dirt.

Geneva pointed down a hill. "The parking lot is down there."

Drake looked. "Is that Ingrid and Allie?"

"Yes."

"Who's that with them, and why are they holding their hands in the air?" Drake asked.

Geneva shook her head. "I don't know."

CHAPTER THIRTEEN

Drake tucked his phone into his pocket and carried the box in one hand as he carefully picked a trail to follow to the bottom of the hill. Geneva moved behind him, almost in his exact footsteps, and unspoken, they moved as silently as possible. Once at the bottom of the hill, Drake handed Geneva the box, then pointed toward the rental car. Geneva nodded her understanding and began making her way to the car.

Drake crept forward. After twenty feet, he noticed Allie nod, which told him she'd seen him. Drake couldn't tell what Allie was saying, but he saw she started speaking rapidly, gesturing with her hands that were still raised at waist-height. Ingrid glanced at Allie, a confused look on her face.

Drake took a few swift, silent strides in their direction, and finally got within earshot when he realized Allie wasn't making conversation, but rather reciting lyrics from an old Queen song. Drake smiled and understood immediately why Ingrid looked baffled. When he got within ten yards, Drake put stealth aside and took off like a bullet, headed toward the man confronting his friends. His footfalls on the stone driveway gave him away, and the man turned the moment Drake got to him. Drake ran into the man's chest, propelling him backward, and falling flat on his back with Drake right on top of him. He recognized Asger, and a flash of steel caught his eye. Drake blocked the knife blow with his arm, grabbed a handful of Asger's hair and drove his head into the ground. Asger's eyes flickered and closed, and his body went limp. Drake waited a few seconds to determine if Asger was playing possum, then got off the prone body, collected the knife, and found his feet.

"We need to go," Drake said.

"You think?" Allie said. "Where's Geneva?"

Drake pointed ahead as they ran. "Already at the car. And she's got a present for you."

Geneva was waiting for the trio, and the second Ingrid unlocked the car, Geneva opened the door and scrambled into the backseat. A few seconds later, her friends joined her. Ingrid started the car, shifted it into gear, and left a rooster tail of gravel as she left the parking lot.

"Here," Geneva said as she handed the wooden box to Allie, who sat next to her.

Allie took the box and inspected all six sides. She tried moving panels and continued until, on the fourth side, one slid away. She gave the box a quarter-turn and moved another piece. Allie smiled and held the box up. "This seems easy enough."

While Ingrid drove through the streets, Allie worked on the box.

"Can we pull over?" Drake asked. "I'm really itching to inspect this car and check if we've picked up another bug."

"Do you want me to help you?" Allie asked, not taking her eyes from her prize.

"No, keep doing what you're doing. How about up there?" Drake asked, pointing to the parking lot of a supermarket.

Ingrid pulled into the lot and found a spot at the far end. She pointed the front end toward the exit and left the engine running while Drake got out and did his inspection. Ten minutes later, he slid back into the passenger seat.

"I didn't find anything," Drake said, scratching his head.

"Need me to take a look?" Allie asked.

"No," Drake said. "Do you have that box open yet?"

Allie slid open another piece, rotated the box, and slid another. Once again, it resembled the back end of a porcupine. She pressed the button inside, heard a click, realized something was released, and lifted the cover from the base.

"As a matter of fact, yes, I do," Allie said. She placed the top on the seat between her and Geneva, then placed the base on her lap and pulled from it a bundle of waxed pages. She carefully undid the seal and discovered several pieces of parchment. "I think this is in Danish," she said, passing the three sheets to Ingrid.

Ingrid studied the sheets, periodically glancing through the windshield to see if she needed to make a fast escape.

"Can you read it?" Drake asked.

"Some yes, some no," Ingrid said. "The first two pages are in Danish; the third appears to be in Old Norse."

"What can you tell us?" Geneva asked.

Ingrid studied the first page again, then read aloud from it. "I'm the only one left in the unit. With luck, I've recovered the asset from the enemy, and although they continue to hound me day and night, I've managed to escape every time. I fear, however, my time is running short. How many times can a man tempt fate? How many times can he escape within the span of a cat's breath? I fear my luck may soon run out. I've transcribed the following page. With my limited resources, I've only been able to translate a few of the symbols. It mentions the tip, but the tip of what I don't know. The tip of the country? The tip of the spear? Perhaps that's it. Supposedly, Hitler is obsessed with the Spear of Destiny, which is rumored to guarantee victory in battle and give its possessor control over the entire world. The spear, if it exists, would be dangerous in the hands of that madman. Still, that's only speculation, and until I can find someone who can decipher the old language, I cannot be sure. All I can do is continue leaving clues behind, for I can't risk being captured by the enemy without leaving a way for someone else to carry on in my stead. I suspect that the enemy may be closer than I care to hope."

Ingrid stopped reading. "That's all there is. Like there's a page missing."

"Do you know where we can get the other page translated? The one you can't read?" Drake asked.

Ingrid smiled. "Of course. We can go to the library."

"Which one?" Drake asked.

"Any library with a proper scanner and Internet access."

Ingrid took a moment to get her bearings on her map app, then located the nearest library and set the directions. She pulled out of the parking lot and turned into traffic. "Ten minutes is all we need," she said.

Geneva turned and looked behind them. "I hope we have ten minutes. How is it that everyone knows where we are? And why, for heaven's sake, are they following us?"

Drake shook his head. "I imagine they're after us because we're on the trail of... whatever it is we're on the trail of. Whatever it is, must be of great interest to Ingrid's friend, as well as whoever the other men are."

"What happened to the other men?" Ingrid asked.

"Hopefully, they're wandering around in the mine still," Geneva said. "A better question is what's going on with your friend?"

Ingrid shook her head. "I wish I knew. I didn't think of asking him while he held us at knifepoint."

"Maybe you'll be on better terms the next time you see him," Drake said.

Ingrid gave him a sour look, then laughed, breaking the

tension. "We'll have to wait and see about that. I'm pretty particular about having conversations after being threatened."

The group rode in silence for the remaining few minutes until, at last, Ingrid pulled into the parking lot of the library. Once again, she found a spot to park where she could make a hasty exit if needed. Rather than everyone going into the library, they decided Drake should accompany Ingrid inside, while Allie and Geneva remain with the car, with Allie behind the wheel and the engine running, just in case they had unexpected company.

"Are you going to watch my six?" Ingrid asked as Drake held the door open for her.

"Of course," he said.

They entered the building, and Ingrid stepped right to the librarian's desk and inquired about a scanner. The librarian escorted Ingrid and Drake to a row of electronics that included a printer that acted as a copier and scanner, as well as a half-dozen computer stations.

Ingrid thanked the librarian, and when the librarian left, Ingrid read the directions on the scanner, laid the parchment face down on the glass, dropped the appropriate number of kroner into the slot, and pressed the green button. The machine roared to life, and a few seconds later, the process was completed.

"Now what?" Drake asked.

Ingrid checked her email and refreshed it until the document came through. When it did, she slipped in front of a computer, accessed her email, and moved the scan into a translator. As the processor did its thing, Drake stood by Ingrid's side, his attention on the library's front door.

"Got it," Ingrid said a few minutes later. She took a picture of the screen with her phone, then cleared the computer's memory cache and rebooted the machine. "Let's go."

"Wait," Drake said, holding her back with an arm.

Drake watched as a man wearing an overcoat entered the library, looked around, then approached the librarian. They had a brief conversation, and then the librarian led the man into the stacks.

"Okay. We can move," Drake said.

He led Ingrid from the library out into the parking lot. Allie slipped from the driver's seat and took her spot in the passenger seat while Drake climbed into the back with Geneva.

"What did you find out?" Allie asked.

Ingrid opened her phone and looked at the photo. "I didn't get a word-for-word translation, but I got enough to know that we need to head to Skagen."

"Where's that?" Geneva asked.

"It's about as far north in Denmark as we can go," Ingrid said. She switched from her email to her maps app and put in the town. "Skagen is on a peninsula at the northern point of the country." When Ingrid zoomed in on the map, the town looked like a cowlick on a head of hair heading out into the sea.

"The tip as mentioned in the letter?" Drake asked.

"That would be my best guess," Ingrid said.

"How long would it take for us to get there?" Geneva asked.

"Around three hours, depending on traffic," Ingrid said.

Allie checked her phone. "It will be eight by the time we get there. Why don't we find a meal along the way, and maybe find a place to sleep? I don't know about you, but I need a nap."

Drake nodded in agreement. "Now that you mention it, you're right. We've been running on nothing more than adrenaline all day, and we could all use a break."

"Should we find a place in town here?" Ingrid asked.

"No," Drake said immediately. "Let's get a little farther up the road. Wherever we end up, we should be in a place with lots of people around."

* * *

Ingrid smelled charred flesh and opened her eyes. To her

surprise, she wasn't snuggled in a warm hotel bed next to her friend, but rather in a makeshift tent. She discovered that the heaviness across her body wasn't a comforter, but sheepskin. Ingrid tossed the hide aside and clambered to her feet. She hurried to the opening, flipped open the hide covering the doorway, and peered out into the camp. Around her was a conflagration like none she'd ever witnessed before. Several of the tents were on fire, as were many of the surrounding trees. She heard a horse nearby. It let loose something that sounded more like a scream than a whinny, then galloped past her, its white mane on fire.

Everything around her was ablaze. Tents, vegetation, animals, people. In the distance, cutting through the black smoke, she spotted movement. A moment later, a sword sliced through the air and the smoke parted, as if cleaved in half. A man came toward her, the largest man she'd ever seen. He rode a horse the approximate size of a baby elephant, and yet the man's feet floated only inches above the ground.

The Viking moved forward. He wore a vest made of an animal's hide Ingrid couldn't recognize. His long, scraggly hair, mustache, and beard were the same dark reddish color as the flames consuming the surroundings around her. Slowly, he approached. When the horse was close enough to nip Ingrid, the Viking stopped. Silently, he parted the vest, and Ingrid saw the torque he wore around his neck. It appeared made of solid gold, but it shimmered as if produced from pure starlight. One side of the torque was a serpent's head, and as Ingrid stared at it, she imagined she saw the forked tongue slip out and back into its mouth. On the other side of the torque was a ship's bow, which raised and fell with each breath the Viking took, looking as if it were out at sea.

The Viking screamed words Ingrid didn't understand, and as he did so, he grabbed each end of the torque. Suddenly, his head got replaced by a blinding pillar of white light that cut a shaft straight into the sky. His scream doubled, then tripled in intensity, and the horse on which he rode burst into flame.

Ingrid screamed. She closed her eyes. A moment later she felt a shove that threatened to tip her over. She opened her eyes, blinking in the darkness, trying to determine where she was.

"Ingrid? Are you okay? You're having a nightmare."

Ingrid moved her hand and placed it in Allie's. "I'm fine," she said, not sure if she was or not.

"Want to talk about it?" Allie asked.

"I don't know. It was a bad dream."

"What about?"

Ingrid tried to remember but couldn't get all the details. "There were horses in it. And lots of fire. That's all I remember."

Allie squeezed her hand. "I'm sorry. Is there anything I can do? Get you some water, or a blanket, or something?"

"No, what time is it?"

The muted light from Allie's phone came on, then died out a second later. "Almost six."

Ingrid pushed the covers aside, rose, and headed into the bathroom. She relieved herself, then washed her hands and splashed a bit of water on her face. When she returned to bed, Allie was sitting up, her back to the headboard.

"What kind of nightmare was it?" Allie asked.

Ingrid smiled, although Allie couldn't see it. "Like I said. I don't really remember much of it. But I'm left with this feeling that something horrible is going to happen in the future."

Ingrid sat in the dark, and when Allie started to breathe rhythmically, Ingrid got up and sat in a chair near the window. She pulled the curtains around her and looked out at the hotel's parking lot. Off in the corner, she could see their rental car, and for a moment, she thought she saw a figure standing next to it. She blinked her eyes twice, and the figure vanished like an apparition.

Ingrid lightly dozed in the chair, and when Allie's alarm

erupted at seven, Ingrid rose, stretched, and popped her back.

"You never got back to sleep," Allie said, more a statement of fact than a question. "What's going on?"

Ingrid brushed it off. "Just my bad dream. I'll be fine. We should get up and get going. I could really go for some pancakes."

Allie remained silent, knowing when to drop an issue.

* * *

"Should we stop for lunch?" Drake asked.

Ingrid checked the clock on the dashboard. It was already three in the afternoon. The pancakes she'd had for breakfast had at first settled like stones in her stomach, but eventually the feeling went away. When Drake asked about food, her stomach rumbled like the ocean waves she could see off to their right as she drove north along the town's main road.

"We'll make this one last stop and then get lunch," Ingrid said.

"Can you believe we've been to four different museums and half a dozen historic sites and have found nothing?" Allie asked.

"I can't believe it's been so easy until now," Ingrid admitted.

Allie reflected on the statement for a moment. "Yeah. We do have an amazing amount of luck following these clues."

"I'll give you the luck since we've had a ton of it, but we still have skill," Geneva piped in from the backseat. "As geocachers, we notice a lot of things that would be overlooked by the general public."

"I'll give you that one," Ingrid said as she pulled into a parking lot.

"What's this place?" Allie asked.

"The Germans used it as a bunker during World War II," Ingrid said. "Now it's a museum."

"Perfect place to hide something from the war," Geneva

said.

"Not really," Drake said.

"That's rude," Geneva said.

"Not really. Think about it. The guy was trying to avoid the Germans, so why in the world would he hide something in a building where everyone there is trying to capture him?"

"That's actually a good point, Drake," Allie admitted.

Drake grinned. "Thank you. There's a virtual geocache near here. Can we grab it after we're done at the museum?"

"Where is it?" Ingrid asked.

Drake checked his phone. "It's to the north of here. About a half mile."

"Sure," Ingrid said. "Let's check the museum first."

Forty minutes later, having struck out at the museum, the friends were walking on the beach with Drake in the lead, heading for a geocache.

"What are we looking for?" Allie asked.

Drake shrugged. "No clue. All I know is that it's a virtual with a difficulty of one and a terrain of two."

Drake passed his phone to Ingrid, who read the description quickly and passed it back to Drake.

"It says all we need to do is include a picture of the object in the background," Ingrid said. "And before you ask, no, it didn't say what object. I imagine we'll find out when we get to ground zero."

"There's something coming," Geneva said, pointing ahead of them.

The group stopped and watched. At first, it looked like a common farm tractor was cutting through the sand, bearing down on them. As it got closer, they noticed the bright blue tractor was pulling what looked like a train car behind it.

"It's a sandworm," Ingrid said as it passed. "You can ride them all the way to the tip of this beach."

"Why aren't we doing that instead of walking?" Geneva

asked.

Ingrid shrugged. "I didn't think of it? Besides, it doesn't stop anywhere but at the end, and that's not where the cache is, right, Drake?"

"Yep. The cache should be just on the other side of this sand dune."

The ground followed a rise, and when they got to the top, they spotted a lighthouse ahead, painted bright white, its tower pointing into the sky.

"That looks just like my dream," Ingrid murmured.

"Did you say something?" Allie asked.

"I said this day is looking up," Ingrid said. "Let's check this out."

CHAPTER FOURTEEN

Drake turned his back to the lighthouse, made sure it was within frame, and snapped a selfie. He took a second to examine the picture before uploading it to log the virtual cache. Geneva, Allie, and Ingrid did the same, although Allie and Ingrid took the picture together and shared it.

"That's done," Drake said. "I'll check to see if there are other caches in the area."

"While you do that, I'm going to take a closer look at the lighthouse," Ingrid said. "Come with me, Allie."

Together, the friends approached the tower. The tall white wooden structure stood on a base of solid rock on a section of the shore that jutted out into the sea. Erosion and time had created a natural spot for the building since the bedrock where it stood loomed fifteen feet above the ground of the surrounding area. As they got closer, they noticed the lighthouse was still in operation and well maintained. It seemed recently painted, and the glass around the top shimmered and reflected the afternoon sun. Four large concrete steps led to the only door.

"I assume that sign means we can't go in," Allie said,

pointing to the sign that hung from a chain blocking the door. There were only two words on the snow-white sign, both blocked and printed in red.

"Your Danish is improving," Ingrid joked.

Beyond the chain, both women noticed the door contained several locks, including a heavy padlock the size of Allie's fist.

"Were you hoping to go in there?" Allie asked. "It doesn't look old enough to house anything from the war."

"No, it doesn't," Ingrid agreed. "It reminded me of my dream from last night. Can we walk around it?"

"Sure."

Ingrid led the way and followed a concrete path, which took the women to the seaside of the lighthouse. There, they found a thick rail fence to protect them from falling into the water. They leaned over the fence, looking out into the sea. The sky was baby blue, broken up only by a crossing seagull looking for food. A breeze created whitecaps farther out, but by the time the water broke to the shore, it only gently lapped against the limestone below them.

"It's pretty here," Allie said.

Ingrid nodded. "And peaceful. Why don't we find a pleasant home by the ocean to live?"

"You live in Boston. Isn't that close enough to the ocean for you?"

Ingrid shook her head. "Not Boston. Or any large city. Somewhere quiet. With a nice beach house."

"Oceans mean hurricanes," Allie said. "I'm not sure I'd want to deal with that threat every year. Seems too stressful for me."

"Okay then. What about a lake? Or a property with a private pond. We can afford to live literally anywhere in the world we want to. So why don't we?"

Allie grabbed Ingrid's hand and gave it a squeeze. "I thought you loved living in Boston. Your parents are there. You like teaching there."

Ingrid nodded. "I can teach anywhere. I could be a substitute somewhere. Or I could give it up. I'd hate to leave Geneva behind."

Allie nodded. "I get it. Of all of us, she's the one living her dream working with the symphony. I'd hate for her to give that up. Have you talked to her about moving away?"

Ingrid shrugged and shook her head. "No. Maybe I just have a case of wanderlust. I seem to get it every time we go somewhere as a group."

"I can understand that," Allie said. "Hey, I get it, too. I have to admit, though, it would be nice to get together with you more than a few times a year."

Ingrid put her arm around Allie and pulled her into a hug. "I'd like that, too. Come on. The others are probably waiting for us."

They walked hand in hand, following the path to the far side of the lighthouse. There, embedded into a boulder, they discovered a large plaque.

Ingrid read it and gave Allie a summary. "A lighthouse has stood on this spot since around the year 1200. Over the years, weather and war have destroyed it. The current base was shored up and modified in the 1920s when they completely rebuilt the lighthouse. They renovated it again in 1951 and completely automated it in 2010."

"Allie! Ingrid! Come over here!"

The women looked at each other.

"What do you think he's up to?" Allie asked.

Ingrid shrugged. "Let's go find out."

They traced their way to the other side of the lighthouse, where they found Geneva waiting for them on the concrete path.

"Where's Drake?" Allie asked. "I heard him calling for us."

"He's down there," Geneva said, pointing to the cliff where the shore met the sea.

"What? Why?"

Geneva emitted a heavy sigh. "I said half-jokingly that he should go down there and check if there are any symbols carved into the rock like we found in the mine. Before I could stop him, he was already halfway down the embankment. A few minutes later, he sent me these."

Geneva brought up Drake's text messages on her phone and passed it to Allie. The first picture showed Drake's view. There appeared to be a small cave on the ocean side of the cliff, and somehow Drake had made his way into it. The picture showed the small, Volkswagen-sized space from inside, looking out to the sea. The second photo showed Drake mugging for the camera, with the cave wall in the background. In the third picture, Drake showed a crude etching of the sunrise over the water.

"Looks like the coin," Allie said.

"That's what I thought. Look at the next photo."

Allie scrolled. The next shot showed Drake pointing a finger, presumably at where he found the marking, which was in the back corner of the cave, obscured by a boulder the size of a mini fridge. Allie noticed quite a bit of graffiti art sprayed on the walls.

"Must be a popular place," Allie noted. "Could the markings simply be more graffiti?"

"No. It was too far back in the cave. I had to turn myself into a pretzel to get in there," Drake said.

Allie turned around and saw Drake approaching them. His jeans' knees were muddy, the rest of his clothes covered in dust, and there was a single leaf stuck to the side of his head by a clump of cobwebs.

"Find anything?" Geneva asked as she pulled the mess from Drake's hair.

"I found the same discolored patch of stone that we found in the mine. I figure it must be some makeshift concrete, because I took a rock and bashed it right open. This was inside." Drake lifted his arm and handed Allie a wax paper bundle.

Without hesitation, Allie carefully opened the bundle.

Inside, she found a section of parchment, and when she undid that, she discovered the missing piece of the map they had already.

"Amazing," Allie said.

"There's something written on the other side," Ingrid said.

Allie flipped the paper over. Everyone standing there recognized the map coordinates. Beneath the numbers, the initials J.L. appeared hastily scrawled on the page.

"Good old Jens. I guess he made it this far," Ingrid said.

"And the courage he must have had to hide this so close to a German outpost," Drake said.

Geneva grabbed Drake's arm and squeezed. "We need to go! They found us again!"

Drake looked up, and Allie and Ingrid spun around. A few hundred feet away and closing the distance quickly were the two strangers who insisted on following them all over the country.

"I'm getting tired of this," Drake said. He grabbed the wax paper wrapping from Allie and shoved it into his back pocket, making sure it was sticking out enough for all to see. "Take the rest of that. I'll meet you back at the car. If I'm not back in an hour, I'll meet you at the hotel we stayed in last night."

Drake took off at a full run, headed toward the two men. At the last second, he turned and headed north to the end of the point. The stranger's friend began chasing Drake, while the stranger kept moving toward the women.

"What should we do?" Geneva asked.

"Um, run," Allie said.

As one, the women sprinted from the lighthouse at an angle away from the man.

Ingrid looked over her shoulder. "He started running after us. Should we split up?"

"Good idea," Allie said. "We'll all meet back at the car."

Allie continued straight toward the parking lot, which she knew was over a mile away, while Ingrid and Geneva veered toward the west. She watched as they ran practically shoulder to shoulder when they split again, with Ingrid moving on a more westward arc, while Geneva headed southwest. Allie glanced in the other direction and realized that the stranger hadn't bothered with the ruse and was in hot pursuit of her.

She ran as hard as she could, her shoes kicking up puffs of sand with every stride she made. Allie hoped the sand would slow down the stranger, but when she threw a glance over her left shoulder, she saw he was making up ground on her. She figured within two minutes she'd be done.

Allie cut across the sand to her right and heard the blare of a horn. Instinctively, she stopped dead in her tracks, turned around, and saw the bright blue tractor of the sandworm bearing down on her. She spun again and threw her hands over her head, ready to be run down, but the tractor stopped before hitting her. Still, it came close enough for her to feel the heat from the radiator penetrate her clothes.

The tractor driver yelled something in Danish that Allie didn't understand. Allie turned around and waved her hands at him.

"I'm sorry! That man is chasing me!" Allie pointed in the direction of the stranger, who was only a few hundred yards away and showed no signs of slowing.

The tractor driver looked to where Allie pointed, saw the man, and waved for Allie to step on the running board of the tractor. She'd barely taken her second foot off the ground when the driver put it in gear and moved away as fast as the machine could go while pulling the train car of tourists behind it. Allie turned, noticing that although it seemed to creep along the sand, it still moved faster than the human trying to catch it. As she watched, the man slowed from a run to a jog, to a walk, then stopped altogether. The man extracted his phone from his pocket and placed a call, never taking his eyes off of Allie.

"Thank you," Allie said to the tractor driver.

The tractor ride took another ten minutes to reach the parking lot, but Allie didn't mind since she didn't have to slog her way through the sand. Once parked, she thanked the driver again, then made her way to the rental car, where she wasn't surprised to be the first to arrive. She moved to the edge of the parking lot, where she sat down in a patch of grass beneath a tree. From her vantage she could keep an eye on the car, and while she did, she removed her shoes and socks, brushed out all the accumulated sand, and put them back on.

When Geneva appeared at the rental, Allie stood, whistled, and waved Geneva over once her friend spotted her.

"Are we the only two back?" Geneva asked.

"So far," Allie said. "I expect Ingrid will show up shortly. It might take Drake another hour to return if he ran all the way to the end of the beach."

"I hope he didn't. I really wish he'd stop taking such risks," Geneva said.

"Have you asked him to?" Allie asked as she corralled a wisp of red hair and tucked it behind her ear.

"We've had this discussion many times," Geneva said. "Half the time I don't even think he knows he's doing it. It's like he acts purely on instinct and doesn't stop for a second to consider his actions."

Allie smiled. "That's Drake for sure. He's been like that the entire time that I've known him. We were geocaching in Florida once, and the cache was on an island about fifty yards into a small lake. Before I knew it, he had stripped down to his shorts and dog-paddled out to that island. When he got back, I asked if he considered the dangers. He asked what could be so dangerous. All I needed to do was point toward an alligator sunning itself on the shore that was only a hundred or so feet away. He looked at me and said 'oh'. Can you believe that?"

Geneva shook her head. "Why didn't you stop him after you saw the gator?"

"By the time I spotted it, he was already on his way back."

"He really needs to start thinking smarter," Geneva said after a pause.

"I suspect he will soon. He's getting older, and they say that wisdom comes with age."

Geneva winked at Allie. "True, but they never say at what age that wisdom comes."

Allie smiled. She clambered to her feet and extended a hand to help Geneva up. "Come on. Ingrid's back."

When they got to the car, Ingrid was sitting sideways in the driver's seat, dumping sand from her shoes like Allie had done.

"You guys have any trouble getting away?" Ingrid asked.

"I never saw anyone," Geneva said.

"Me neither," Ingrid said.

"The one guy followed me for a while. I thought he would catch me, too, but I hitched a ride with a sandworm. He made a call. I can only assume it was to his buddy," Allie said.

"I hope Drake is okay," Geneva said. She turned, facing the park, hoping to spot him jogging toward them at any minute.

"Depending on how far he ran out, it could take him a while to get back," Ingrid said. "Get in and get comfortable. He did say that we should give him an hour."

Ingrid finished cleaning her shoes as her friends got in the car. As Allie studied the map fragment, Geneva and Ingrid passed the time with meaningless chatter. Soon, that died off, and all three women sat in silence for an extended period.

Allie checked her phone. "It's been eighty minutes. He should have been here by now. Maybe we should go looking for him."

"That's a bad idea," Ingrid said. "There's three miles of sandbar out there, and I don't know how wide it is. That would be like trying to find him in a place bigger than Central Park. We'd be better off waiting for him to come to us."

"As much as I hate to, I agree with Ingrid," Geneva said. "He said he'd meet us at the hotel if we didn't hear from him by now. Let's go there and wait."

"Okay, you're both right. Let's go," Allie said.

Ingrid started the car, placed it in gear, and touched the gas. It inched forward a foot, then another car skidded to a stop right in front of her. She hit the brakes hard enough to jostle everyone in the vehicle. Ingrid, thinking it was a tourist jockeying for a good parking spot, waited for a few seconds for the other car to move. It didn't. Instead, she watched as Asger and a woman left the vehicle and headed toward her door. Ingrid switched gears, hoping to back up, but as she was about to, a black BMW stopped behind her.

"What's going on?" Geneva asked.

Ingrid double-checked that she'd locked the doors. "I'm not sure."

Asger moved to the driver's window and rapped on the glass with his knuckles. "You should come out here and talk to us."

Ingrid stood firm. "No. Let us go."

Asger turned around and said something to the woman. She handed him her phone. He glanced at it, then turned the screen to Ingrid. Through the glass, she saw a live feed of Drake on his knees. His hands looked tied behind him, and the stranger held him by his hair.

"We can play this one of two ways. My colleagues can hurt him, or you can get out of the car and talk to us," Asgar said. He sneered, then returned the phone to the woman.

Ingrid turned off the car, unlocked the doors, and got out.

"Your friends, too," Mette said.

Allie and Geneva joined Ingrid in the parking lot.

"You will hand over the treasure," the woman said in Danish.

"We haven't found a treasure," Ingrid said.

The woman stepped forward and slapped Ingrid's face.

"Lies. I've been tracking you. You aren't tourists. You've found the treasure."

Ingrid felt her cheek grow warm, but didn't move to rub it or show any other signs of weakness. "We've found a series of clues. Nothing more. Each clue leads only to another clue. I told you the truth when I said we haven't found a treasure."

"You found a clue at the lighthouse?" Mette asked.

Ingrid glowered at the woman, but didn't answer.

Mette held up her phone again. On screen, the stranger pulled Drake's head back and held a knife to his throat.

"Yes," Ingrid said.

"I told you to check there," Mette said to Asgar, her words coming out surrounded by a shell of irritation.

Asger didn't reply.

Mette turned her attention back to Ingrid. "You will get the treasure and deliver it to me. Your friends will stay with me until you return."

Ingrid shook her head. "I need them. There have been puzzles and things to solve. We work as a team. I wouldn't be able to do it alone."

Mette considered the point for a moment. "Fine. Your friends go with you. Your boyfriend, however, will stay with me. If you don't get me what I want, you'll never see him again. Also, Asger will join you as your fourth, just to make sure you don't get any ideas about calling the police or staging some half-baked rescue attempt." Mette checked her phone and noted the time. "You'd better get going. You have twenty-four hours. I'll be in touch."

Mette returned to her car and pulled it forward to give Ingrid room to leave, then returned to the group and addressed Asger. "Listen, if they find something, you call me. If they give you any trouble, you call me. If they contact anyone, you call me. Do you understand? You do nothing you don't clear through me first."

Asger nodded, then walked around the car and slipped into

the rental's passenger seat. "Come on. You're wasting time standing there."

CHAPTER FIFTEEN

Ingrid took her place behind the wheel of the rental, and Allie and Geneva climbed into the backseats. Ingrid started the car and reached for the shifter when Asger stopped her.

"Wait," he said. "You behind me in the backseat, get out of the car."

Allie hesitated for a moment while Ingrid unlocked the doors, and she left the car. Once she was out, Asger opened his door and left the car.

"Wait until I'm in the car, then get in the front seat," Asger said to Allie.

Allie stood still as Asger slid into the seat next to Geneva, and Allie jumped in the front.

"Now, drive," Asgar ordered. "And don't any of you try to do anything. I'm armed."

Ingrid looked at him in the mirror; her eyes flashed red in anger. She was about to say something, but then realized she had missed the question that Allie had asked.

"What?"

"Can I put these coordinates into your maps?"

Ingrid dropped her eyes, entered the password on her phone and handed it to Allie. Allie entered the numbers into the map and pushed the button to calculate the route. After a few seconds of calculations, the voice gave Ingrid the first of the directions, which, in essence, led her out of the parking lot.

Ingrid studied the route for a moment and set the phone down next to her.

"Where are we going?" Asger asked.

"Aalborg," Ingrid said, her voice hard.

Asger nodded and grinned in the backseat. "Aalborg. Of course. We're probably headed to Lindholm Hills. Why aren't we moving?"

Ingrid passed an icy glance in the rearview mirror and feathered the gas to pull out of the parking space. Slowly, she moved through the parking lot to the entrance and pulled out onto the road heading south.

"How long will it take to get there?" Asger asked. He waited ten seconds for an answer, which he never got. With a quick move, he reached over, grabbed Geneva by the hair and pulled her down so that her head was in his lap. There was a reflection of light on metal, and a second later, he held the point of a knife over her left ear. "Pull over to the side of the road. And do it slowly."

Ingrid saw what was going on in the backseat, eased off the gas, and pulled over as ordered.

"I don't think you understand how this is going to go," Asger growled. "I'm in charge of this expedition now. Not you. Not any of your friends. Me. When I ask a question, I expect a response right away. Otherwise…"

Asger pushed Geneva deeper into his lap and moved the knife lower. Geneva let out a scream when the sharp edge contacted the flesh of her earlobe. "Do we have an understanding, or do I have to drive this knife into her brain?"

"Stop!" Ingrid yelled. "You're in charge! Let her go!"

"Tell me what I want to know first. Hurry, my arm is getting tired."

Ingrid picked up her phone and found the answer. "Ninety minutes. Maybe more depending on traffic."

"No," Asger said, shaking his head. "Ninety minutes. Not a second longer, or your friend and Van Gogh will have something in common."

Asger moved the knife, and with his other hand pushed Geneva away from him. Once released, she slid as far away from him as she could against the car door. Her hand moved to her ear, and when she looked, she saw her fingers were red with blood.

"Here, take these," Allie said, turning around in her seat to pass Geneva a handful of napkins they'd collected.

Geneva hesitated, looking at Asger.

"Go ahead, take them," he said.

Geneva reached forward enough to grab the napkins and moved quickly back to her door. She took one off the pile, folded it in half, and pressed it against her ear. She held it in place for a few seconds, then looked at it, noticing the saturation. Geneva dropped the napkin to the floor and replaced it with a fresh one, applying more pressure than she had initially.

"Here's the deal," Asger said plainly. "If you don't cooperate with me, you can get the blade or get a bullet, depending on your offense and my mood. Also, don't forget that we have the man, and if you ever want to see him again, you won't get on my bad side. I need only to make a phone call, and your friend will suffer a tragic boating accident out in the bay. Do you understand?"

Silence enveloped the car.

Asger held up his knife, the edge still discolored with Geneva's blood. "I asked a question, and I need an answer."

"I understand," Ingrid said.

"Good. What about the rest of you?"

"I understand," Allie said.

Asger looked at Geneva, her hand still pressed against her ear. She gave him a tentative nod.

"Good," Asger said. He took a moment to wipe his blade against Geneva's jeans. Once it was clean, he closed the knife and slid it into his jacket pocket. "We can go now. Remember. Ninety minutes. Not a second more."

Ingrid waited for an opening in traffic and pulled back onto the road. She checked the map app and noted the time.

"I don't think ninety minutes is going to be enough," she said to Allie.

"I guess you'd better not waste any of it," Asger said without giving Allie a chance to respond.

Ingrid checked her speed and, since traffic seemed fairly light, she pushed the accelerator until they traveled ten miles over the speed limit.

"Do you think Drake's okay?" Allie asked.

"No talking," Asger said.

"I'm worried about my friend," Allie said.

Asger leaned forward in his seat and grabbed a length of Allie's hair and pulled it until she squealed.

"I said no talking." He held on to her for almost fifteen seconds before letting her go. When he did, Allie adjusted her seat, moving as far forward as she could.

Ingrid, meanwhile, concentrated on the road. She'd only been on Route 40 a few times, but she'd always enjoyed it, especially the stretch of highway that ran parallel to the beach and gave her an unobstructed view of the ocean, but this ride was much different. The hum of the tires on the roadway sounded calm and rhythmic, but to the three women inside the tiny rental car, every mile felt like a countdown, a clock ticking ever louder, headed for the inevitable explosion of a time bomb.

Ingrid gripped the steering wheel so tightly her knuckles turned white. Sweat clung to her neck, so she flipped on the air conditioning and adjusted the vents to blow the cool air directly onto her face.

Allie recognized Ingrid's discomfort and leaned slightly in her direction. "Wiggle your fingers," she whispered and sat upright.

Ingrid smiled at the suggestion. It was a common thing Allie said anytime she was with someone who seemed stressed about driving in rain, snow, heavy traffic, over high bridges, or whatever triggered the driver's anxiety. Ingrid took her suggestion and without releasing the wheel, wiggled the fingers on both hands. Eventually, she felt comfortable enough to remove her right hand from the wheel completely and rested it on her lap. Her eyes flicked to the rearview mirror, pretending to check traffic, but instead she focused on Asger.

Asger sat behind Allie, legs spread wide, elbow propped against the window. To anyone driving by, they could have looked like any other group of travelers heading for unknown destinations. But his posture wasn't casual. It seemed calculated. His right hand hung low, close to the waistband of his jacket, occasionally brushing against something she could not see. He'd already produced and used the knife. Ingrid didn't know for sure if he actually had a gun. She knew Denmark had highly restrictive gun laws, but that didn't mean it was impossible to buy a firearm.

"Keep your eyes forward," Asger said when he caught Ingrid staring at him. His voice was icy, calm, and firm.

Ingrid forced herself to look forward again, waited for a full minute and looked in the mirror again, this time focusing on Geneva. Geneva sat rigid, staring out the window, each breath carefully controlled. Her ear had stopped bleeding, and she no longer held the napkin there, but Ingrid spotted a bit of paper stuck to Geneva's ear, attached to her earlobe like an earring.

Now they drove in total dread, the silence between them disrupted only by the sound of the tires rolling along the asphalt.

Thirty minutes had passed since Asger first climbed into the car, and the sign on the road welcomed them to the city of Frederikshavn. They had already passed through a half-dozen small towns, and Ingrid did the same at each, speeding as fast as she dared along the open road, slowing as she went through the town before stomping down on the accelerator once through. She feared her process wouldn't work in the much larger city they'd reached, and she realized she had to get through the entire town to pick up the road she needed to get to Aalborg.

"Ingrid! Stop!" Allie yelled.

Ingrid focused on the road in front of her. Caught in the daydream she was in, she hadn't seen the vehicles ahead of her stopping because of construction. She slammed on the brakes, causing everyone in the car to lurch forward, and she stopped mere inches from the back bumper of a white delivery van.

Asger leaned between the seats to see what was going on. "Just keep driving," he said.

"We're in construction," Ingrid argued.

"I don't care. Go around it, go over it, go through it. The clock doesn't stop simply because the road did. Remember, we have your friend."

Ingrid glanced in the mirror and caught Asger's eyes. He looked serious. She shifted her focus behind them and put the car in reverse. The auto behind them honked the horn, showing Ingrid was about to hit them, so she stopped. The traffic ahead stayed still, so she turned the wheel to the left, hoping to go around it. She put the car in gear and let off the brake and hit it again when a construction vehicle appeared next to her.

"It's one lane ahead," Allie said to Ingrid. "We have to wait our turn."

Ingrid watched as car after car passed them on the left.

"Tick Tock," Asger said.

Ingrid sighed. She backed up slowly until she felt her rear bumper kiss the car behind them, then turned the wheel all the way to the right. She barely touched the gas, and the car lurched as it crawled up the curb. Carefully, she navigated until the entire car was on the sidewalk. Ingrid pressed on the gas, hoping the construction had dissuaded pedestrians from taking that route.

Allie put her hands out, preparing to brace herself. "Ingrid! We're going to crash!"

Ingrid noticed the cement truck ahead, also on the sidewalk, as it dropped its load into a large hole in the road. "I got it."

Ingrid drove forward another fifty feet and spun the wheel, bounding off the sidewalk and into the parking lot of a bank. She parked haphazardly across four marked spots, then studied her phone for an alternate route. Satisfied she had one, she hit the gas and exited onto a cross street. She drove on for almost a mile when she slammed on her brakes again, this time as a school crossing guard stepped into the road and held up a stop sign on a stick.

"We need to get moving," Asger said.

Ingrid glared into the mirror. "Screw you. I'm not running down a bunch of schoolchildren."

Asger shrugged. "Your choice. I hope your friend doesn't pay the cost of your decision."

Ingrid turned her attention back to the road. The last of the children was almost to the curb. Although the crossing guard was still in the middle of the road, Ingrid peppered the pedal and swerved around her. Ingrid watched as the crossing guard shook a fist at her, and slowly a plan formed in her brain.

She turned three corners and found herself on the E45, the road that would take them all the way to Aalborg. Once out of the city, Ingrid wet her lips, glancing at the speedometer. She was going ten kilometers over the speed limit.

"Too subtle," she whispered to herself. She pressed the pedal harder and watched as the speedometer needle climbed ten higher.

"Keep it steady," Asger said.

Ingrid nodded and watched as the needle jumped another

five kilometers higher.

Asger leaned forward suddenly, the cool metal of the knife glinting faintly. "I said to keep it steady."

"She's nervous. That's all. You've given her an impossible timeline," Geneva said without turning her head.

Asger's eyes narrowed. "You're all nervous." He leaned back again. "Good. That means you're paying attention."

Ingrid placed all her attention on the road and prayed to the highway gods, then, like a miracle, she saw it a half mile ahead. The white cruiser with the blue lights on top was sitting at a crossroads. Ingrid hoped he was running radar, and her heart hammered so loud she was afraid Asgar could hear it.

She did something dangerous. Ingrid drifted slightly across the center line, only enough to make the car twitch.

Asger was suddenly alert, knife in hand. "What the hell was that?"

Ingrid's voice shook. "There was something in the road. An animal, I think."

Asger leaned forward, his breath hot against her neck. "You hit anything again, and I'll make sure your friend back here gets another hole in her head. Understand?"

Ingrid nodded, but kept her eyes on the cruiser. As she got closer to the intersection, she made her move and flashed the headlights twice in succession, then did it again. A silent SOS. She prayed the officer would notice.

She passed the car without slowing down.

A second later, the lights on the cruiser flashed to life, and a siren sounded.

Asgar turned, saw the cop, and cursed under his breath. "Keep calm. Just keep driving."

The blue lights filled the car's interior, and the siren wailed, echoing through the rental.

"All right, pull over," Asger said. "But if you say one word, I'll cut your friend." He pointed the blade at Geneva, who froze like glass.

"I got it," Ingrid said. She turned the wheel and pulled onto the gravel shoulder.

The police cruiser stopped behind them, engine idling. After a delay that seemed like hours, Ingrid saw the officer step out and walk toward them, hand resting on his holster, professional, but not yet hardened. He approached the driver's window.

"Smile," Asger whispered.

Ingrid rolled down the window about two inches. Her voice came out hoarse. "Hello, officer," she said in Danish.

"Is everything okay? You swerved back there."

Ingrid hesitated, knowing she couldn't say what she wanted. Her mouth was dry. She blinked hard to fight off the tears of frustration.

"Sorry. There was an animal in the road."

The officer's eyes moved past her to Allie, then to the back seat. He frowned slightly. "Everyone all right in here?"

"Yes, we're fine," Asger answered.

The officer looked at Geneva, then at Allie. "What about you two?"

"Oh, I'm sorry, sir," Ingrid said. "They are American. They don't speak Danish."

The officer studied them. The silence was too long. His gaze went back to Ingrid. "Driver, could you step out of the car for a moment?"

Asger's voice dropped to a hiss. "Tell him no."

Ingrid's head turned slightly. "Do I have to?" she whispered to the officer.

"Yes," he said.

Asger straightened and moved closer to Geneva. "You say a word," he whispered, "and your friend is done."

Ingrid opened the door slowly, her legs trembling as she stepped out. The sunlight hit her face, blinding her for a moment.

The officer smiled faintly at first. "I just want to make sure everything's all right." He glanced at the car again. "Your passengers seem a little nervous."

Ingrid chuckled. "They all hate the way I drive."

"Can I have your license?"

Ingrid didn't understand the command for a moment, then retrieved her wallet from the car. She opened it and passed her license to the officer.

"You're American, too. I wouldn't have guessed it. Your Danish is perfect," the officer said, taking the documentation.

"My parents are Danes," Ingrid explained.

"Where are you staying in Denmark?"

Ingrid fished another card out of her wallet. "Here. You can contact me here if you have questions."

The officer read the card and was about to speak when Ingrid interrupted him.

"Of course, we're not there now, but I wish I were. Call there," Ingrid said.

The officer didn't move. He didn't react at all, but then she saw it — a small tightening of his jaw.

"Stay right here, please," the officer said. He turned and walked back to his cruiser.

"Get in the car," Asger ordered.

"He told me to stay here," Ingrid said.

"Get back in the car or your friend dies!" Asger shouted. He slid closer, pinning Geneva against the door, and a second later, the knife point hovered just above her right eye.

"Ingrid," Geneva stammered.

Ingrid looked in the officer's direction, then into the back seat. Not really having a choice, Ingrid climbed back into the driver's seat.

"Drive," Asger ordered.

Ingrid did as she was told, and with a spray of gravel, moved back onto the highway and hit the accelerator. She looked in the mirror, expecting to see the officer on her tail, but he hadn't moved.

"Go faster," Asger demanded.

Defeated, Ingrid complied.

In the patrol car, the officer watched as Ingrid sped away. His adrenaline kicked in, and he wanted to follow, but realized something wasn't right about the entire ordeal. He studied Ingrid's driver's license for a moment, then peered at the business card she'd given him. Finally, he made a decision, grabbed the handheld radio, and clicked it on.

"Base, I need you to put me through to Inspector Louise Jensen."

The officer rattled off the phone number from the card, set it down on the passenger seat next to Ingrid's license, and waited for the call to connect.

CHAPTER SIXTEEN

Ingrid kept her foot on the gas pedal and her eyes on the rearview mirror, expecting to see the police pull in behind her. Actually, she hoped in silence that she would crest a hill and find the entire road blocked by at least the police, and even better, the Danish Army, if only to get Asger out of their hair and put together a plan to save Drake. Surprised at not seeing anyone other than a random car going in the opposite direction, Ingrid kept heading for Aalborg.

"Do you have any idea of where the coordinates are taking us?" Allie whispered.

Ingrid checked the mirror, noticed Asger was looking out the window, and handed Allie her phone. Once in hand, Allie skipped ahead on the map app and followed the pink line to the endpoint.

"It says we're going to someplace called Lindholm Hills," Allie said, hitting the button to recenter the screen before handing the phone back to Ingrid.

"Of course, Lindholm," Asger said. "Just as I guessed. I should have thought of that myself."

"What is that?" Allie whispered to Ingrid.

"I can hear you," Asger said. "It's a major Viking burial site, and a former settlement. Part of the site dates back to the fifth century. Excavations started in the late 1800s, and a major excavation went on in the 1950s. Oh, yeah, that would be the place for a Viking horde of treasure. They've found remains of villages and hundreds of graves there. Vikings abandoned the settlement around 1200, and then the whole thing got buried by the drifting sands of time."

Allie turned in her seat. "And that's where you think we'll find the treasure?"

Asger grinned. "Why not? Over the last sixty years, they've found gems, coins, jewelry, and glassware. Lots of things. You can see some of the items recovered at the museum they have on site. Of course, once we've completed our business together."

"What if we find nothing? What if the trail runs cold?" Allie asked.

"How can it?"

"You said yourself this is a major excavation site. What if they already found everything, and it is already sitting in a museum somewhere? It could be the treasure got recovered decades ago."

The grin left Asger's face, replaced by a sneer. "That would be unfortunate for you, especially for the man."

Allie glanced at Ingrid, then turned her attention to the view in front of her.

Ingrid followed the highway and soon entered the city. Warned by Asger not to draw attention to them, she played it safe, followed the speed limit to the digit, and made turns whenever her map directed her to. She turned right onto a simple two-lane road and followed the blacktop for a mile until she spotted the sign for the historical site. Ingrid pulled into the parking lot, found a spot closest to the road, and shut down the car. Just as she cracked open the door, an alarm on her phone destroyed the silence.

"What's that?" Asger demanded.

"Relax. Just a timer. Ninety minutes." Ingrid unlocked her phone and shut off the alarm.

"Everyone out," Asger said.

The women followed the order. As they stood outside, Allie gave Geneva's ear a once-over and determined it would heal fine and most likely wouldn't leave a scar.

"Where to now?" Asger said.

Ingrid checked her phone to see where the coordinates led her and pointed toward the south. "That way, about a third of a mile."

"Go. No one leaves my sight, understand?" Asger said.

"Yeah, yeah, we got you," Ingrid said. She eyed her phone and began walking. She led them across the parking lot and found a dirt path that led through a line of beech trees. They walked for a hundred yards, the elevation climbing with every step, and entered a clearing at the top of a grassy hill. From where they were, they could see open pastureland to their left, and a view of the city of Aalborg and the banks of the Limfjord to the south.

"Wow," Allie said, focusing on the land in front of them. Across the summit of the hill there were countless graves marked by stone arrangements set in ovals, triangles, or outlines of boats. "This is amazing."

"Don't get distracted. Keep moving," Asger said.

Ingrid checked her phone and walked another two hundred feet before coming to a stop. "This is the spot. Where the coordinates take us, give or take five feet."

The group stood in the middle of a grave featuring a ship's outline.

Asger looked around and turned over a couple of stones. "There's nothing here."

"Sorry. We brought you here. Now give Drake back," Allie

said, stepping toe to toe with Asger.

There was a flash of steel, and Asger held his knife before Allie's eyes. "Back off. There's something here. Find it, or I'll start carving you up like your Thanksgiving capons."

Allie held her position for a moment. "Turkey." She stepped back only when Ingrid grabbed her shoulder and forced her to move.

"Think about Drake," Ingrid said. "There must be more. What's on the map?"

Allie produced the map halves and handed them to Ingrid. Ingrid held the two pieces together and stared at them for a few minutes. She turned over the newly acquired piece and compared the coordinates on the sheet to the ones she'd entered into her app. They matched.

"Wait a second," Ingrid said. "I sense something odd about this paper."

Ingrid handed the larger sheet to Allie and traced her finger on the smaller sheet. "There appear to be indentations. Anyone have a crayon or a pencil on them?"

"Are you serious?" Geneva asked.

Ingrid crouched, laid the parchment flat on the ground and took a fistful of earth and spread it over the sheet. She tamped it down lightly, leaned over until her nose almost touched the page, and blew away the loose dirt. Left behind were faint brown markings, now visible on the paper.

"Holy cow," Allie said, handing Ingrid the other sheet. "Do this one, too."

Ingrid placed the sheet where the two pages aligned, then repeated the process. When she finished, everyone could see the full page of rune markings gently carved into the delicate parchment.

"What does that say?" Geneva asked.

"I wouldn't even guess. I'll have to translate it," Ingrid said.

Before she could pick up the pages, Asger swooped in and

plucked them from the ground.

"Thanks," he said. He studied the papers for a moment, then nodded his head and grinned. "I can take it from here. You go back to your hotel. We'll release the man when I find the treasure. If I need you, I always know where to find you." He turned and began walking toward the museum in the distance.

"Hey," Ingrid protested, rising from her position.

"Let him go," Allie said, grabbing him by the arm.

"He's got the pages!"

"So what? I've got a picture."

Allie showed Ingrid her phone and the snapshot she'd taken over Ingrid's shoulder.

"You are a sneaky one," Ingrid said.

"Can you figure this out?" Allie asked.

"Sure. Let's get out of here, though."

The three jogged to the car, got in, and Ingrid drove them to a coffee shop not far away. While she worked on the translation, Allie and Geneva sat by, nursing cups of tea and trying hard not to disturb Ingrid while she worked, jotting notes on the back of order slips they'd borrowed from a waitress.

An hour later, Ingrid dropped her pencil on the tabletop and took a drink of long-cold tea. "I get why the coordinates didn't work," she said.

"The coordinates are fine," Allie said.

"Yes. How did you guess?" Ingrid said, pushing her empty cup aside.

"Classic geocacher mistake. We tend to search horizontally, not vertically. The thing is underground, isn't it?"

Ingrid nodded.

"Do you know how to get to the spot?" Geneva asked.

"Not yet, but I'm sure we'll have to go back to the site," Ingrid said. "Also, I found some riddles here we need to figure out."

"Riddles? For what?" Allie asked.

"I don't know. But they must have a purpose. Otherwise, why bother writing them out?" Ingrid said.

"Okay," Allie said. "What do you have?"

"It says, solve the riddles of the Gods. Four answers will unlock the path you shall travel through the labyrinth."

Geneva's eyes widened. "Riddles. I hate riddles. What do they have to do with anything?"

Allie shrugged. "We won't know until we figure them out. What's the first one?"

Ingrid rotated the paper so everyone could see it. She pointed to a crude figure. "I'm not an artist, but you can see it clearer on the phone." She brought up the photo on Allie's phone and zoomed in.

"It looks like a wolf's head," Allie said. "What's the riddle?"

"Although I surrendered an eye, my insight stays clear. My two familiars whisper news from lands afar. God of knowledge, what name do I bear?"

"Familiars? Who has familiars?" Geneva asked.

Allie took her phone back and ran a quick search. "Odin. His wolves were Geri and Freki. He also had a couple of ravens."

"You know, I've seen that wolf symbol before," Ingrid said. From her back pocket, she took the computer rendering she'd gotten at the university. She unfolded it, pressed it flat, and scanned it until she found it. "Here," she said, pointing. "I assumed it was simply another town, but apparently there's more to it than that."

She followed the image from a path that began at the wolf's snout and moved it until it intersected with more paths. "It looks like when we find the entrance, we go this way."

"Step one is Odin's path?" Allie asked.

Geneva looked over the sheets. "Four riddles, four corridors. Odyssey through the labyrinth?"

"It could be," Ingrid said. "Should we keep going?"

Allie nodded. "Of course. What's next?"

Ingrid pointed at the sheet. Next to a crudely drawn hammer, she'd written another line.

"From mountain to meadow, I thunder and rage. Lightning is mine, and monsters I cage. Whoso wields my power, steers storms and fights fate. Name me, my mighty relic and weapon of weight."

Geneva's face lit up. "That's Mjolnir. Thor's hammer. Drake loved those movies."

Ingrid nodded. "Mjolnir gave Thor his strength. It shattered mountains and scattered giants."

"And crushed that rock giant into pebbles," Geneva added. "Is there a hammer on the paper, too?"

Ingrid moved the map to the center of the table so everyone could see it.

"There it is," Geneva said, pointing to the picture. Several spokes came off of the circle that Odin's path led to, and each had a small glyph at the beginning of the line. One had Mjolnir. Allie traced the path with her finger and ended when it came to another junction.

"Two down, two to go," Allie said. "What's next?"

Ingrid returned to her notes. Next to the next line, she'd drawn a crude feather. "In love and war, I travel the sky. My necklace grants favor; my chariot can fly. Valkyries heed, and warriors fear, from beauty and secrets my name will appear."

"What was her name in the movies? Freezer something? Thor's mom?" Geneva said.

"Frigga," Allie said. Allie turned to her phone and made a few queries. "That can't be the answer, though. They made Frigga up. In mythology, Thor's mom's name is Fjorgyn, and she has nothing to do with a necklace. Hold on."

"While she's doing that, let's look for a feather on the map," Ingrid said to Geneva.

"I got it," Allie said. "The answer is Freyja, the goddess of love and war, gold, and sex. Sounds like a fun lady. She has a necklace named Brisingamen, and rides a chariot pulled by two cats. Freyja also has a pet boar and has a cloak made of falcon feathers, which allows her to transform into a falcon."

"She does sound cool," Ingrid admitted. "I don't see any feathers on this map, though."

"Me neither," Geneva said.

"Okay, then, look for necklaces, chariots, cats, or boars," Allie said. "If it holds close to the other answers, it should branch off of that junction."

"Here it is," Geneva said, putting her finger on the item. "It looks more like a pig than a boar, but I'll bet that's it." Geneva followed the path as it wound around the paper and ended at another junction.

"Not done yet," Allie said. "What's the last one?"

Ingrid studied her sheet. "This one has a snake next to it. Is there one on the map?"

Geneva looked at the glyphs exiting the junction. "Not one. Four. What's the riddle?"

Ingrid read. "With words and with wiles, I alter the thread. Shape-shifting slyly, betrayal I spread. From Asgard to Midgard, my jokes spark dread. Who am I, the maker of trouble and fear?"

"That one's easy," Geneva said. "Loki. He's the god of mischief and chaos. Thor's half-brother."

"That's right," Allie added. "They called him the Trickster. He was into shapeshifting and double-crossing."

"Great. But how do we know which of these paths to take?" Geneva asked.

Allie dove into her phone. "Okay. More on Loki. Some things he shape-shifted into include a salmon, a mare, a fly, and an old woman."

"A fly?" Geneva asked. "Why would someone change into a fly?"

"That's better than a salmon. I would think becoming a fish would limit one's ability to travel around," Allie said.

"It would also increase the chances of being caught for someone's dinner," Geneva said.

"Would you two stop joking around?" Ingrid asked, becoming annoyed.

"Relax, Ingrid, we're just having a little fun," Allie said. "Hey, is this one a fly?"

Geneva leaned over the sheet. "It's really hard to tell. It could be a fly, or it could be an inkblot."

"Is there another symbol that would imply a different route?" Allie asked.

"Not that I can find," Geneva said.

"Let's go with this one, then," Allie said. She traced her finger along the path, looping around the paper, and stopped when it ended.

The last symbol had no junctions. Instead, it looked like a square with circles intersecting each side.

"That was anticlimactic," Geneva said. "What do you suppose it is?"

"We won't know for sure until we find it," Allie said.

"I hope there aren't any more riddles involved," Geneva said. "I hate riddles."

Allie smiled. "Come on, at least these were easy ones."

"That's true," Geneva conceded. "Although I wonder why. If this path leads to a great treasure, you'd think they'd want to hide it better. Or not leave any map behind at all."

"Who knows why they did what they did."

"And what about the curse? What kind of curse are we looking at?" Geneva asked.

Allie and Ingrid were silent for a moment, then Allie turned back to her phone. A few minutes later, she addressed her friends. "There are a ton of magical items in Norse and Viking history, such as Thor's hammer, but I didn't find many that claimed to be cursed. I did find a couple, though. There's a ring cursed by a dwarf that will bring ruin to all who possess it. And there's a sword called Tyrfing that, once drawn, will always draw blood and must be unsheathed and fed once a year. There's also a torque, which is a kind of magical necklace that will bring great power to anyone who wears it. Although, with that one, it says anyone misusing the power will get consumed in a column of fire."

"Gosh, I can't wait to find the treasure," Ingrid said. "Sounds like whatever we find will be fun to deal with."

"I don't think there's anything left to find," Allie said. "Based on what Asger said about this area being excavated over the course of decades. It would really surprise me if we found anything at all. Of course, there's something else we need to figure out, too."

"What's that?" Ingrid asked.

"How do we get Drake back, and how do we find a treasure without getting ourselves killed?"

"That's a brilliant question," Geneva said. "I certainly don't want to get sliced again."

"Do you think your friend will get Drake killed if we bring in the police?" Allie asked.

Ingrid shook her head. "I can't say for sure. The Asger I knew as my childhood friend isn't the person we're dealing with today. Honestly, I can't even tell you who this person is. Would he have Drake killed? Your guess is as good as mine, but based on how fast he pulled that knife on Geneva, I'd bet it's more of a possibility than not."

Allie considered her words, then nodded. "Do you think he can figure out those riddles on his own?"

Ingrid nodded. "Probably. He's not a stupid man, but he doesn't have this." Ingrid pointed to the printed map, which they'd traced the labyrinth route on based on the answered riddles.

"All he needs to do is turn the parchment over, and he does," Geneva said.

Ingrid picked up her cup, realized it was empty, and set it down. "True. But I'm not sure that would help him in every case. The one we have went through a computer and got scanned, analyzed, and augmented. That blob we thought was a fly? On his copy, he'll have more blobs than just this one. We'll have to go in and hope that he makes a wrong turn or two."

"I think we need to go for the treasure," Allie said. "If we get to it first, we at least have something to bargain with to get Drake back. Otherwise, he's probably done for. Agreed?"

Ingrid and Geneva nodded.

"Before we go back to the site and start, you should give your friend a call," Allie said.

"Asger?" Ingrid asked.

"No. That police inspector."

CHAPTER SEVENTEEN

Ingrid drove through the parking lot slowly, searching for any signs of Asger.

"Where do you think he is?" Ingrid asked.

Allie crinkled her nose. "As I see it, there are only four possibilities. He's in the museum, he's on the hill, he's searching underground for the treasure, or he's gone."

"I doubt that he's gone," Ingrid said. "He doesn't have a car, remember. Besides, I doubt he could have figured out all the riddles quicker than we did, or made the connection to the map on the other side of the parchment."

"You're probably right. What do you want to do?"

"I think we should be as discreet as possible and try to find the entrance to the labyrinth." Ingrid said as she crept past the museum a third time. She moved the car to the end of the lot and parked in an empty section, hood of the car pointed toward the exit.

"How much time do we have?" Ingrid asked.

"One hour and fifty minutes," Allie said.

"Do you wonder whether we gave ourselves enough time

before Geneva calls in the local police?"

Allie shrugged. "Your guess is as good as mine. Who knows what the scale of the map is. We won't find out until we get down there."

Ingrid turned off the car. "You mean *if* we get down there. I'm not sure where to check for the entrance."

"I have an idea about that. Let's go into the museum first."

The women got out of the car and moved swiftly to the building. While Ingrid bought entry tickets for the duo, Allie scanned the area trying to catch a glimpse of Asger.

"I don't see him anywhere," Allie said once they'd gained entry.

"Let's take a quick look around," Ingrid said.

The pair moved through the museum quickly, but stopped at the door before entering any room to make sure Asger wasn't in it. They rushed past several displays highlighting the life of the Vikings in the area, including the jewelry they wore. They also passed several exhibits that told the story of the North Jutland region from ancient times to the era when Vikings settled the land. When they arrived at the last exhibit, the women stopped at the exit door.

"He's not in here," Ingrid said.

Allie nodded in agreement. "I didn't spot him either. I noticed a display that should help us. Come on."

The friends backtracked through several rooms until they arrived in a room dedicated to the excavations done in the area over several decades. In the center stood a large three-dimensional relief of what the settlement looked like in Viking times. Hanging on the wall was a map of the burial sites, featuring not only the visible sites but also the underground ones discovered by ground-penetrating radar.

"Does any of this seem familiar?" Allie asked.

Ingrid nodded and removed the map from her pocket. She unfolded it and compared the map to the graves in the display.

"I don't know. I don't really see anything that aligns. Hold on. I've got an idea."

Ingrid stepped back a few paces and took a photo of the wall.

"What are you doing?" Allie asked.

Without looking up from her phone, Ingrid offered an explanation. "I'm loading the picture of the cemetery here into a graphics software along with a picture of the map I got. Now I'm adjusting it so they're the same size and away we go."

Ingrid turned her phone around so Allie could check the result.

"That's a mess with the way they overlay each other," Allie said.

Ingrid glanced at the screen. "Whoops. I forgot a step." She turned the phone around and fiddled with some buttons as Allie watched. "Now I just need to change the transparency of the map image, and that should help. There. Got it."

Ingrid handed Allie her phone, and Allie noticed the graves stood out in a stark black font while Ingrid rendered the map slightly behind it in a dull gray. She found the path from the first riddle and traced it backwards where it ended near the edge of the road to the east.

"Is this the entrance?" Allie asked, pointing at the spot.

"I believe it is," Ingrid said. "Let's go find out."

As they watched for Asger, the duo made their way out of the building and walked across the parking lot. When they reached the end, they continued on a well-maintained patch of grass that ran parallel to the beech trees until they met the road.

Ingrid checked her phone. "I estimate it's about fifty feet that way," she said, pointing to the south.

Allie followed a few steps behind, and eventually Ingrid slowed and then stopped. Three feet to their left was the road, and a foot to their right was a shallow culvert meant to prevent erosion of the landscape or damage to the pavement.

"I don't think this is right," Allie said.

"Well, it was an estimate," Ingrid said. "Remember back in the old days of geocaching when the coordinates would take you within thirty feet? Think of this like that. We'll spread out and look around."

"I don't think we need to spread that far. If the entrance was farther that way, they would have destroyed it when they laid the road or the ditch. My guess is we need to go up the hill." Allie pointed to their right, where the terrain took a vertical jump and the beech trees thrived.

"Makes sense. I'm right behind you," Ingrid said.

Allie looked at the hill, then began her ascent. The first eight feet weren't too bad, but then she needed to lean into the hill and grab for any branches she could reach to help pull her up. She'd made it twenty feet before she turned around and sat down, her back against a tree.

"Are you okay?" Ingrid asked.

"Yeah. Leg hurts a bit. I'm not made for these steep climbs anymore."

"Ever since that fall in Arizona, right?" Ingrid asked.

Allie nodded. "Sorry. Give me a minute to rest, and I'll keep moving."

Ingrid squeezed Allie's shoulder, then passed her, climbing higher up the hill. A few moments later, she stopped. "Hey, Allie? I think I found something."

Allie exhaled, and with an audible huff, got to her feet. When she turned, she saw Ingrid only a few yards ahead, stopped where a tree had grown horizontal. Struggling, Allie lumbered on until she met her friend.

"What's up?" Allie asked as she stopped, bent over, breathing hard.

"I think there's a cave here," Ingrid said, pointing to a spot where the tree met the hill.

Allie leaned in. "I don't see anything."

Ingrid moved closer to the hill, struggling against the tree boughs. As she got closer to the earth, she needed to step around a handful of exposed roots. She lifted herself over the trunk, then disappeared from view.

"I'm right. There is a cave here."

"Great," Allie whispered to herself. "I'm right behind you."

With difficulty, Allie did her best to follow Ingrid's path through the branches, over the roots, and as she slid over the trunk, she passed headfirst into a small cavern, not much larger than the interior of their rental car. Other than a tree root breaking through the ceiling and small scattered stones, the space looked empty.

"There's nothing here," Allie said. "Let's go back out and try somewhere else."

"No," Ingrid said. She activated the flashlight on her phone and studied the far wall. "It makes little sense for it to be anywhere else." Her beam stopped. "Here. Take a gander at this!"

Allie took a deep breath and moved farther into the void. She followed Ingrid's beam of light, which settled on a crude carving that resembled a wolf's head.

"Okay. You win."

Ingrid grinned, then looked around. She spotted a baseball-sized rock, wrapped her hand around it, and pummeled the carving. After the third strike, the wolf crumbled away, and on the fifth, she broke through the wall.

"How did you know it would do that?" Allie asked.

"I'd hoped, based on the false walls Drake found earlier. Come on. It's time for an adventure!"

Ingrid, on her hands and knees, disappeared into the darkness with Allie begrudgingly behind her. Once through, the cavern opened and they could stand up.

They both activated their phone flashlights and moved forward sixty paces until they came to a round room with several exits.

"Where to?" Allie asked.

Ingrid checked her phone, then selected the exit second from her left. "This way."

As they walked, the ground sloped downward, and with every fifty feet, the temperature dropped a degree. Allie let Ingrid lead and followed a few paces behind, trying hard to forget where she was.

"Are you okay?" Ingrid asked without halting.

"Not really," Allie said. "I should have stayed behind instead of Geneva. You know I don't enjoy being underground."

Ingrid stopped and faced her friend. "You know as well as I do you wouldn't have traded places with Geneva. With what she's been through, she's already on edge. It was best to leave her at the coffee shop, and once the inspector gets to her, Geneva can bring in the cavalry and save the day."

Allie nodded. "You're right. I'll just pretend we're above ground, wandering around at night, which is why we can't see."

Ingrid wanted to respond, but Allie held up a finger, stopping her.

"Shh," Allie said.

The two women stood in the dark, waiting and listening. Ten seconds turned to twenty, and then they heard voices echoing in the tunnel behind them.

"Asger?" Allie whispered.

Ingrid nodded. "Probably. We should get going."

Ingrid turned and headed away while Allie stood still for a moment. As her light followed Ingrid's departure, she clearly saw Ingrid's footprints in the light layer of dirt on the passage floor. Allie took a deep breath and rushed to catch up with her friend.

"We've got a problem," Allie said. "We're leaving footprints that will lead him right to us."

"There's nothing we can do about it until we reach the next junction," Ingrid said. "Let's figure out what to do then. Come on, we'll do double time."

Without waiting, Ingrid sharpened her pace to a swift walk, her light bouncing off the walls as she moved. Five minutes later, they entered another room, this one smaller than the first. It held four exits, and while Ingrid checked the map to see which they should take, Allie removed her windbreaker.

"Second from the right," Ingrid said.

When Ingrid moved into the corridor, Allie stepped in right behind her. Walking backwards, she swept the earth with her jacket, obscuring their footprints.

"Do you think that will fool him?" Ingrid asked, looking back.

"I don't know. It's better than nothing. Hopefully, he's as ill-equipped for this adventure as we are. Lead on."

Ingrid continued the journey, and after seventy feet, Allie gave up the ruse, opting for speed instead of stealth. As they rushed through the corridor, they could sense the curvature of the walls on either side. Several times they came to openings that led to other corridors, but since they didn't match Ingrid's map, they disregarded them as fast as they encountered them.

Fifteen minutes later they arrived at the third junction. After checking the map, Ingrid selected the middle of five potential exits, and Allie used her coat to wipe away the footprints for the first thirty feet they walked. The number of routes doubled as they went on as the slope continued to decline, and the temperature fell.

The corridor opened into the last room — a large room, twenty feet in diameter with eight exits. Ingrid studied the map for a moment, then selected the first corridor on her left. The passage snaked to their left, then right, then left again, and for every fifty feet they walked, they passed the entrance to another corridor.

"How are you doing back there?" Ingrid asked.

Allie considered her feelings for a moment. "Actually, I'm

not too bad. I have a bit of claustrophobia closing in, but as long as the passage is as roomy as it is, I'm okay. I'm pretending that we're working our way through a haunted house."

Ingrid giggled. "You would find a haunted house less scary than this?"

"Ha!" Allie scoffed. "Of course. There's nothing in a haunted house that could hurt me."

"Not even one filled with vampires, werewolves, and assorted monsters?"

"Correction. Those are people playing monsters. Not actual monsters, and I've had enough training to fight my way out of a building against a bunch of ghouls."

"Point taken," Ingrid said after giving it a moment's thought. "Hey, do you see a light up ahead?"

The women stopped. They held out their flashlights and focused on the tunnel ahead. The lights flickered on and off, as if they were heading into a den of fireflies.

Side by side they resumed their journey, and a few steps later, they crossed the threshold into the last room. The flooring changed from bare earth to porcelain tile, and the women entered cautiously, their steps echoing on tile softened by centuries of dust.

"Wow. I'm guessing they never found this place," Allie said. As they looked around, they saw the room glittering with precious metals. They spotted shields engraved with runes, axes inlaid with shimmering stones, torques, rings, and helmets shaped like dragon heads.

At the room's center sat a pedestal, upon which rested an ornate box, which was inlaid with precious stones.

"This is incredible," Ingrid said, approaching the box.

"Be careful," Allie warned as Ingrid reached for the treasure.

"I'm sure it's okay," Ingrid said as she placed her hands on either side of the box. She attempted to lift it, but it stayed locked to the pedestal. She tried to move it again, but couldn't. "It's stuck."

Allie stepped to her side and tried to shift the box. It didn't budge. She let go of the box and leaned in to examine one of the ornate cat paws that served as feet.

"There's a little slit here," Allie said. She checked the other foot and found the same. "What about on that side?"

Ingrid moved to the opposite side of the box. "Same thing over here. What do you suppose that's about?"

Allie dug in her pants pocket and extracted the coins Geneva had given her. She slid a coin into one slot, pushed it in, and heard a soft click. She passed two of the coins to Ingrid and pushed the fourth coin into place. Allie removed the box easily from the pedestal.

The box sat on a raised section of stone, and once removed, the stone sank into the pedestal. A second later, the wall behind them rumbled. With a great clatter, a shield dropped to the floor, followed by a section of wall that broke away, revealing another tunnel. A spear slid out of place and fell across the door they'd entered by.

"I hope that's the way out," Allie said.

"Oh, you won't need to worry about an exit," Mette said as she darkened the doorway. "Once I clean this place out and take this box, you can be a part of this tomb forever."

Allie inspected the woman. She didn't appear to have a weapon, but that appearance was deceiving when she lifted her arm, exposing the handgun she had casually hanging at her side. She barely noticed Asger as he moved beside the woman.

"Put the box on the ground and step aside. Asger, get in there and take care of them," Mette said.

Asger hesitated. "What do you mean by that?"

Mette huffed. "You idiot. Take my gun and finish this."

"You mean kill them?" Asger asked.

"Of course. We don't want any witnesses."

"You told me only to watch them, scare them if necessary

until we found this place."

"They look scared, don't they? You've done a good job. Finish them and let's get out of this dank place."

Asger looked at the gun in her hand, then at the women cowering on the far side of the room.

Mette glanced at Asger and slapped him across the face. "You've got two choices: take care of them and get your fair share of the riches, or you can join them in this lovely burial chamber."

The two got into a stare-off.

"Before you decide, you should know that I found out about your contingency plan. I know that if you don't contact your sister every forty-eight hours, she'll go to the authorities. Trust me. If you don't carry this through, or if anything happens to me, she won't live that long."

Asger looked at his shoes, then took the gun.

"Asger," Ingrid stammered. "You don't have to do this."

Asger reached forward, grabbed the spear blocking his path, and pulled it to release it from the wall. When he did, there was a rumble, and dirt fell from the entrance ceiling. Asger and Mette took steps back, and a moment later the ceiling gave way and collapsed, blocking the doorway with a ton of rock.

Inside the room, Allie and Ingrid needed to shield their eyes from the dirt cloud thrown into the air. Once it settled, they stared at where the entryway used to be.

"Are you okay?" Allie asked.

"Yeah. Are you?"

Allie nodded.

Allie turned around and approached the fallen wall behind them. She picked up the shield and set it aside to give them room to pass.

"Should we arm ourselves?" Ingrid asked.

Allie considered it for a moment, then nodded. "That's a good idea."

From the weaponry displayed on the walls, Ingrid selected

a short ax, while Allie found a dagger with a jeweled handle.

"Think that will cut anything?" Ingrid asked, nodding at the knife.

Allie felt the edge with the meat of her thumb. "Maybe melted butter. You must admit; it does look scary and a bit badass."

Ingrid giggled. "Come on. Let's get out of here."

Allie slipped the dagger blade into the back pocket of her jeans and picked up the box. "That's the best idea I've heard all day."

CHAPTER EIGHTEEN

Allie and Ingrid stepped over the wall debris into the dark passage beyond. The air tasted stale, of clay and old water. Ingrid's flashlight flickered twice, throwing shadows across the dirt walls.

"What's going on?" Allie asked.

"My battery is going dead. You wouldn't happen to have a power bank on you, would you?"

"No, turn it off. I still have fifty percent battery left. Hopefully, we'll be out of here by then."

Ingrid's light went out. Before it did, its glow showed rugged walls that narrowed the farther forward they ventured.

"I changed my mind," Allie said. "I should have swapped spots with Geneva."

"Yeah, me too," Ingrid answered.

"Stop! Don't move!" Allie said as she halted.

Ingrid finished her half-step. Her shoe sank an inch into the mud. "Why?"

Allie crouched low and brushed her fingers along the floor. The soil seemed different, and she could smell rot from underneath. "There's a hollow spot here."

"Hollow as in 'secret tunnel,' or hollow as in 'fall until we hit a bunch of pointy spears'?" Ingrid asked.

"I'm guessing the second one," Allie said. "Step back a second and let me borrow your ax."

Ingrid swallowed hard, slowly lifted her foot, and moved back a step. Allie took the ax from her and pressed the handle in several spots on the ground before them. On the third poke, the soil collapsed inward where they were about to step, revealing a pit of dark emptiness beneath.

"Damn," Ingrid stammered, a bit above a whisper. "One more step and we'd be…"

"Gone," Allie finished. She leaned closer to the edge and held her phone out. The pit stretched several feet down, its bottom lined with sharpened wooden stakes, blackened with age. "You were right about the spears, though."

"Who builds something like this?" Ingrid asked.

Allie shrugged. "People who don't like trespassers. It's too bad we can't go back the way we came. It's a shame the door collapsed behind us."

"So, we keep moving forward," Ingrid said. "If there's a pit here, there has to be a reason for it. There must be an exit somewhere in this direction."

"Probably," Allie agreed. "Let's deal with this first."

Allie stepped up to the pit and skirted the edge carefully, moving sideways, her shoes squelching in the muck. Eventually, she made it to the far side and held the flashlight steady while Ingrid followed in her footsteps. Once clear, they continued on.

They didn't know how long they'd been underground. The section of the labyrinth they'd stumbled into didn't appear on Ingrid's map. Instead, it was a web of hand-dug corridors with roots curling from the ceilings and moisture seeping in through the dirt walls.

After what seemed like an eternity later, Allie's hand

brushed along the wall and she noticed a change in the texture, which was something she expected as she checked for additional traps. She stopped and examined the point closer and found a vertical seam where the packed earth felt smoother.

"Here," she said.

Ingrid moved to her side. "You found something?"

Allie nodded. "This section got reinforced. Someone sealed a passage here."

"With dirt?"

"I think it's packed clay." Allie dug her dagger into the seam, chipping away. The light shimmered on something behind the hole. "There's a wooden door here. Help me."

The two women worked together, scraping and clawing until a crude wooden plank appeared. A few minutes later, the makeshift door gave way and fell to the ground, splashing into a shallow puddle of muddy water.

They stepped through the doorway into a narrow passage. Here, the builders had reinforced the narrow walls with rough timber beams. The air seemed cooler, fresher.

Allie walked a few paces. The tunnel sloped upward.

Ingrid nearly laughed with relief. "We're going up!"

"Careful," Allie said. "Traps don't stop simply because the floor changed." She felt better, almost hopeful as they climbed, following the incline.

After a few hundred yards, the walls widened into a low, rounded chamber. At the far end, half buried in the dirt, a circular stone disk jutted from the wall. As the friends approached, they saw engravings of carvings that looked familiar to both of them.

"That looks like a mechanism," Ingrid said.

"Or a door," Allie said. She wiped sweat from her brow. "Give me the coins."

Ingrid put the treasure box on the floor, removed the four coins from the legs, and passed them to Allie. Allie flipped one coin over so it was facing up, and compared the disks in her hand to the slots on the door. She noticed the sea serpent, a sunrise, the spear, and the trident carvings were almost identical. She placed each coin into its matching slot and found each one fit perfectly. There was a stone knob in the center, and she turned it gently, listening. A click echoed through the chamber, then another, deeper one behind the wall.

Allie smiled faintly. "It's working."

She continued turning the knob, and suddenly the stone disk shuddered. Dust rained from above, then the wall cracked open down the middle, revealing a narrow passage filled with a faint, cool breeze.

Ingrid took a deep breath. "Fresh air."

Allie grinned. "And better yet, an exit."

Allie collected the coins, then they squeezed through the opening, crawling on hands and knees until they reached a slope of loose soil. Daylight shimmered faintly above.

"Keep moving," Allie said, pushing Ingrid upward. "I can't tell you how badly I want to be out of here."

Ingrid clawed her way through, dirt tumbling around her, until her hand broke through into open air. She dragged herself into the open, coughing, and turned to pull Allie out after her. The sky above was blinding blue. The two women lay side by side in the grass, gulping lungfuls of fresh air.

Ingrid took off her pack, rolled onto her back and watched a bird fly over. "We made it."

Allie wiped dirt from her face with her T-shirt. "Barely. Remind me never to go underground again."

"Right," Ingrid said, sitting up. "Next time, Geneva and Drake go."

They shared a weak laugh before Allie looked toward the tree line. "We should move. If my internal compass is working, I'd guess that this exit put us near the fields to the west of the museum."

"How far to the car?" Ingrid asked.

"A third of a mile. Perhaps a little more."

They stood, gathered their things, and began walking. Mud streaked their clothes, and the treasure box hung heavy in Ingrid's pack. Neither noticed the pair of binoculars glinting in the distance, nor the figure lowering them with a satisfied smirk.

The pair followed a dirt road through the heather that led into a shallow valley. When they came out on the far rise, they saw the rental car sitting in the museum parking lot, right where they'd left it.

"Think we should turn this stuff into the museum?" Ingrid asked as she popped the locks and opened the door.

"Not yet," Allie said. "I want to make sure we've rendezvoused with Geneva and found Drake first. After the inspector slides handcuffs on Asger and whoever that woman was, we can turn over the things we found." Allie patted the dirt off her jeans before sliding into the passenger seat. "I'm never digging again."

"Noted," Ingrid said, climbing in. She checked the mirrors, started the engine, and pulled out of the parking lot, heading toward Aalborg.

"I'm a little surprised Geneva isn't here with the police, or Asger isn't here waiting for us," Ingrid said.

"I was thinking the same thing," Allie said.

For a few minutes, there was nothing but the hum of tires and the smell of sunbaked soil. The labyrinth already seemed like a fever dream with its mud walls, stale air, and the whisper of shifting dirt. Now there was wind, sky, and motion.

Allie leaned her head back and closed her eyes. "I can't wait until this is over. I would like to find some geocaches and get some ice cream."

Ingrid didn't answer.

"Is there anything you're looking forward to showing us? We haven't seen your family's farm yet."

Ingrid's gaze stayed fixed on the rearview mirror. "We're

being followed."

Allie straightened and looked at her friend. "You're sure?"

Ingrid nodded toward the mirror. "That's Asger's car. Two behind us. It's been on us since the last turn."

Allie craned her neck. "I see it."

Asger kept his distance, gliding smoothly along the road. Two figures sat inside, shapes indistinct behind the glass.

"Are you sure they are following us?" Allie asked. "It could be a coincidence." She didn't sound convinced of her own words.

Ingrid pressed harder on the accelerator and passed a sedan. Asger sped up as well, attempting to catch up with her.

"Not a coincidence," Ingrid said. "What should I do? Head to the coffee shop and pick up Geneva?"

"Geneva. Right. Hold on." Allie dug her phone out of her pocket and placed a call to her friend. She talked for a little more than a minute when her phone died. She pulled it away from her ear and stared at it, as if that would get it to recharge.

"Geneva's with the police. She's at a police station, but doesn't know where. She's waiting for your inspector friend to arrive."

"Geneva didn't give you any sign of where she was?" Ingrid asked.

Allie shook her head. "She said something about a huge language barrier, then my phone died. Where's the charger?"

"Forget the charger. What do we do about Asger?" Ingrid asked.

"Try to lose him while I try to get back in touch with Geneva," Allie said. She rooted around in the console looking for her charging cable.

They hit the main road and merged into traffic along with a pair of trucks, a motorcyclist, and a family sedan. Asger had caught up with them. Ingrid saw he was wearing sunglasses, and the woman behind him was talking wildly into a cell phone.

"Hey, why is your friend following us, and who is that

woman?"

Ingrid shrugged as she navigated a roundabout. "I don't know the answer to either of those questions. Why don't we stop and negotiate with them? Give them the box, and they'll give Drake back to us."

"Do you trust them to follow through on their end of the bargain?"

Ingrid considered it for only half a second. "No. Not really."

"Let's find Geneva and the inspector. After that, we'll make a plan to get Drake back. In the meantime, hit the gas."

Ingrid pressed the pedal, and the landscape blurred past. Fields gave way to the low outskirts of Aalborg. The road widened into asphalt, and Asger inched closer.

"Hold on," Ingrid said.

She cut hard onto a side road lined with poplars, gravel spraying. Asger followed. Ingrid gunned the engine, the little car shaking with effort.

"Left ahead," Ingrid said, reading the signs. "Toward the harbor."

"Great idea," Allie said. "Hopefully, there will be crowds and witnesses there."

They pressed on for minutes, passing warehouses, shipping yards, and old brick facades converted into offices. The car bounded over a pothole. Behind them, Asger still followed, unwavering.

Allie looked in the side mirror. "Only two of them. Asger is driving. Clearly, the woman's in charge."

"I gathered that in the tunnels," Ingrid said. "That stare she has."

"Creepy stare."

"Focused stare," Ingrid corrected. "Like she already knows how this ends."

"No," Allie said. "Like she knows how she thinks it will end. Let's prove her wrong."

Ingrid smiled and slammed on the brakes. Asger swerved, nearly rear-ending them. Ingrid swung the wheel right, darting onto a narrow service road between two warehouses. She sped up again, tires screaming.

"He's still back there," Allie yelled.

"Good."

"What do you mean by that?"

"I think I know where to take them."

They burst onto the main waterfront road; the Limfjord glinting beyond the road. The late-afternoon sun was harsh, the sky streaked with thin clouds. Fishing boats bobbed along the docks, and gulls scattered as Ingrid tore past.

Allie braced herself. "Tell me you have a plan."

"I have a concept of a plan," Ingrid said.

As Asger's car pulled alongside, the engines snarled in unison. The woman in the passenger seat rolled down her window. She shouted something they couldn't hear.

"I think she's threatening me," Ingrid said.

"Don't give her the satisfaction," Allie said.

Ingrid jerked the wheel, sideswiping Asger's car enough to send sparks flying. Both cars wobbled before regaining control. Horns blared from other cars around them.

The woman leaned out and shouted. "Pull over! Now!"

"Screw you!" Ingrid screamed.

The woman pointed her gun out the window. Ingrid spotted it and hit the brakes. When Asger did the same, Ingrid stomped on the gas and surged forward, leaving him in the dust. She raced into the heart of Aalborg. Bounding over cobblestone streets, scattering pedestrians. They shot past the coffee shop where they'd last seen Geneva without slowing.

Ingrid turned sharply toward the harbor district, down a slope leading directly to the waterfront promenade. The tires squealed, brakes shrieked, and yet Asger followed, fishtailing on the slick pavement.

"The police are going to love this," Allie said.

"I hoped they'd be here by now," Ingrid said.

Ahead lay the end of the road, the open quay, then water.

"Um, Ingrid, that's the fjord."

"I see it."

"Then stop!"

Ingrid pulled the handbrake. The rental spun sideways, skidding to a stop just short of the edge. Asger screeched to a halt behind them, blocking their retreat.

Asger stepped out of the car. The woman followed, gun in hand, her expression showing equal parts irritation and frustration.

"Get out," she called in English. Her Danish accent sounded clipped but precise. "Slowly."

Ingrid lifted her hands and stepped out of the car. Allie did the same.

The woman gestured toward the car. "Where is the box?"

Ingrid and Allie hesitated. Asger stepped closer.

"Now," the woman said.

Allie's mind raced. No traps, no ancient mechanisms. Unarmed. But she'd spent half her life in problem-solving situations that started with no apparent way out.

Allie raised her voice slightly. "You followed all this way for a trinket box?"

The woman's eyes narrowed. "You have no idea what that is worth."

"I'm getting that impression."

Asger spoke for the first time. His voice was deep and steady. "Just hand it over, Ingrid, and you both walk away. No one gets hurt."

"What about our friend, Drake?" Ingrid asked.

Asger hesitated. "We can have him here within the hour. Just give us the box."

Allie whispered to Ingrid. "They're lying."

"I know," Ingrid said. Louder, she asked, "And if we don't?"

The woman smiled. "Then you disappear, along with your friends."

Allie took a breath, steadying her hands. "You should have said that sooner."

"Why?"

"Because now," Allie said, glancing past them, "you're out of time."

A shout erupted from behind Asger and Mette. Blue lights flashed against the warehouse walls.

"Police! Drop your weapons!"

The woman spun, cursing. Asger grabbed her arm, and they bolted toward their car as officers poured from two cruisers, weapons raised.

"Get down!" a cop shouted.

Ingrid and Allie dove behind their car. Gunfire cracked. They were warning shots only but enough to send Asger speeding away down the quay.

Allie peered over the hood. "You planned that?"

"Not exactly," Ingrid said, watching Asger vanish into the side streets. "But I'll take the help."

Police swarmed the scene, shouting orders, checking the area. One officer approached them.

"Are you two all right?"

Ingrid nodded. "Fine. Just tourists who took a wrong turn."

The officer frowned at the skid marks on the pavement. "That's one hell of a wrong turn."

Ingrid managed a tight smile. "Long story."

He nodded and turned to his radio.

Allie leaned close. "We're not done, are we?"

Ingrid's eyes fixed on the direction Asger had gone. "No. They'll hide somewhere close. A loading zone, maybe in a warehouse. We can follow the police chatter and find them before they regroup."

Allie stared at her. "You're serious."

"Completely. Just because you are ex-military and Drake is an ex-cop, that doesn't mean that I don't have any experience with this stuff."

"Where did you get it?" Allie said.

Ingrid winked. "Watching old Clint Eastwood movies."

The police lights still pulsed against the walls when Ingrid nudged Allie toward the crowd.

"Now," Ingrid whispered.

They slipped between two parked vans as officers moved to cordon off the quay. Within seconds, they were just two more bystanders in the confusion.

Ingrid exhaled. "We just walked away from an active crime scene."

Allie's voice was low. "That's better than trying to explain why we have a jewel-encrusted treasure box along with Viking weapons in our rental car, none of which we legally own."

"Good point," Ingrid said.

"How do we find them?" Allie asked. "The police will probably have roadblocks up."

"They won't get far by road," Ingrid said, scanning the docks. "My guess is they'll hide until the heat dies down."

"The police are going to cordon this entire area off, including us and our rental full of evidence," Allie said. "We need to get out of here."

Ingrid nodded. "Okay. Let's get the car first, then see if we can turn the tables on Asger."

They found their rental car where they'd left it. It sat half-blocked in by a police van, and although a bit of crime scene tape was wrapped around the side mirror, it seemed intact. They watched from the shadows, waiting for a policeman to appear, but none did.

"They must all be wrapped up in the search," Ingrid said. "Let's get out of here while we can."

They ran to the car and got in. Ingrid started the vehicle, then rolled down the window to remove the yellow tape.

Ingrid checked in the mirror. "We'll go slow, no lights, and try to pretend we're not fleeing an active investigation."

The cops were making their way west, so Ingrid slowly drove east until they cleared the area, then slipped away from the scene. They crept along the waterfront. To their left, the black water of the Limfjord reflected the city's lights.

"Stop," Allie said suddenly. "Look!"

Ahead, Asger's car sat parked beneath a loading crane. Its headlights were off, but the license plate light glowed faintly.

"That's them," Ingrid murmured. "How in the world did they get through the dragnet?"

Allie shrugged. "They must have backtracked somewhere or fooled the cops somehow."

They coasted to a stop behind a stack of containers. Through the windshield, they saw movement. The woman got out of the car and spoke rapidly into a phone, pacing like a leashed dog.

The friends strained to listen. Mette's voice was sharp, controlled, and echoed off the building next to her. "Police interference. We'll secure the item soon."

Then, quieter, "No, they won't survive the next time. We'll need to move before sunrise. The entire shipment leaves at six, including the treasure they have."

Allie leaned closer to Ingrid. "They're smuggling something."

"Or someone," Ingrid said. "Maybe Drake is with them. Why in the world would they be waiting here? Why didn't they leave?"

Allie inspected the Volkswagen from afar. "Their getaway has a flat tire."

They watched as the woman finished her phone call and then got back into the car. The minutes ticked by, and soon another set of headlights approached the vehicle and parked right beside it. The woman got out of Asger's car and climbed into the other. As the car pulled away, Ingrid saw Asger behind the wheel as he headed toward the nearest road.

"They switched cars. What should we do?" Ingrid asked.

"Let's follow them for a change," Allie said.

CHAPTER NINETEEN

Ingrid stayed behind Asger's car at least a hundred yards during the entire time she tailed them. For over an hour, she kept her eyes focused on the taillights as they weaved through the streets and into the dark of night. She expected to have to drive all the way back to Skagen, since that's where they'd captured Drake, but she was surprised when Asger pulled onto a dirt road south of Frederikshavn. Since they were the only two cars on the road, Ingrid held back and let Asger get a quarter mile ahead of her before she resumed her pursuit. When Asger pulled onto a long driveway, Ingrid pulled over to the side of the road and shut off the engine.

From their position, they spotted the distant glow of shimmering lights spilling from the front window of a farmhouse. Based on the peeling white paint on the exterior, the sagging porch, the one shutter hanging crooked from the front window, and the waist-high grass in the yard, it looked as if the house had sat deserted for some time.

Asger and the woman had entered the house over an hour ago, and Ingrid and Allie sat in the car waiting for them to come out again.

"I've had enough of waiting. I'm going in," Allie said, unbuckling her seatbelt and reaching for the handle.

"Are you sure that's a good idea?" Ingrid asked.

"No. But I don't have another one. At the very least, I'd like to check if Drake is in there."

"I'll come with you," Ingrid said.

"No, try to get ahold of Geneva first. If you can, have her bring the police out here and let's finish this thing."

Ingrid hesitated and nodded.

Allie slipped out of the car and closed the door as silently as she could. She walked halfway down the driveway until she came within fifty feet of the house, then slipped into the tall grass and headed for a corner. Flat against the house, she inched herself toward the nearest window, squatted a few inches below the level of the sill, and looked in. The room was dark, and based solely on the ambient light coming from the living room, empty.

Allie duck-walked under the window, and hung next to the house until she came to the next window. This room had light streaming from it, so she assumed this room was occupied, but she needed to determine by whom. Luckily, there was a heavy curtain on the side nearest to her, but rather than try to look through the glass, she took her phone from her pocket, activated the camera, and held it up high enough to clear the level of the sill. She snapped a series of pictures and backed away from the window.

Once she was out of sight of those in the house, Allie checked the pictures. Inside were four people sitting around a card table with a leaning leg. She recognized them all: Asger, the woman with the determined stare, and the two men who had chased them all over Denmark. She flipped through multiple photos of the same thing, then in the last one, taken when she'd moved her arm from the window, she noticed Drake, tied up and lying on the floor.

Allie backed away from the house and returned to the car. She opened the door and slid into the passenger seat.

"Drake is in there," Allie whispered. "So are Asger, the women, and two other men."

"What are they doing?" Ingrid asked.

"I don't know. All I have are the pictures I took. They were talking about something, but I couldn't hear them clearly through the window. Oh, and they were speaking in Danish."

Ingrid shifted slightly and exhaled. "So, if Drake is really in there, what's our play? Should we wait for the police?"

"Did you reach Geneva?" Allie asked.

"Yes. She put a captain on the phone. The inspector hasn't arrived yet, and they won't move until she gets there. It may take up to an hour."

"And then another hour until they get here?" Allie asked.

"Maybe. Unless they send over some local cops," Ingrid said. "I gave them good directions of where we are and even included the coordinates."

Allie smiled. "Great idea. They're not only for geocaching but are also handy in emergency situations." She giggled nervously and became serious again. "Two hours is a long time. Anything might happen by the time help arrives. They could leave or do something bad to Drake."

"Or to us," Ingrid added.

"Right. Or to us," Allie agreed. "Unless we back off from here and move down the road, or into town."

"You don't want to do that, do you?" Ingrid said.

Allie paused, then shook her head. "I think we should do something now."

Ingrid sighed. "We might get ourselves killed. She still has a gun, you know, and those other men could have guns as well."

"We could get Drake killed if we don't do anything. They seem to want this treasure pretty badly, and that is our best leverage."

The wind carried the sudden sound of chatter from the farmhouse, a rough, careless sound that made the hair on the back of Ingrid's neck prickle. She imagined Drake trussed up like a Thanksgiving turkey in some dark room. Her stomach twisted.

"Okay," Ingrid whispered. "We do something. I hope you have a plan."

Allie looked toward the house. "Almost." She remained silent for a while, then smiled. "Got it. You go around to the back and make a lot of noise. When everyone gets distracted and goes to check what's going on, I'll slip in through the front and grab Drake. Then we'll meet back here and head for the city."

"Great. But what if they spot us? Or they split up and don't leave Drake alone?"

Allie considered it for a second. "Then we run."

"Got it. Strong plan."

Allie shrugged. "It was the best I could do in the moment." "Let's try it anyway," Ingrid said. "What's the worst that can happen?"

Allie put up a finger and wagged it in front of Ingrid's face. "Let's not go there. Come on."

The women left the car, and they moved together to the house's corner. When they reached the farmhouse, Allie signaled for Ingrid to stop. Allie pointed at the front window, the only one with a faint orange glow coming from it.

"That's where Drake is," Allie whispered into Ingrid's ear.

Ingrid nodded.

Allie pointed at herself, then the ground, then pointed at Ingrid and motioned around the house. Ingrid got the message. Allie would sit tight until the commotion started.

Ingrid left Allie's side and headed toward the rear of the property. There was a line of apple trees she needed to pass through, and she did so quietly. Every sound, be it a distant owl cry or the creak of a branch swaying in the wind above her, seemed too loud. Ingrid's heart thudded in her chest as she took each tentative step. She moved forward another inch, her foot connecting with a fallen fruit. Her foot rolled, slipped beneath her. With a grunt, Ingrid fell to one knee. Ingrid froze, expecting all the people to come out, checking on the noise. Thirty seconds stretched to a minute, and then beyond. No one came rushing from the house, so she quietly got back to her feet and moved on.

Ingrid's nerves were singing by the time she reached the back door. The old hinges groaned when she pushed it open, the sound too loud in the quiet. She froze, breath held, listening.

Nothing.

She stepped into the kitchen. The old farmhouse smelled of dust, dampness, and something pungent she couldn't identify. She crept down a narrow hallway lined with old frames missing photographs, toward the muffled voices. Her heartbeat hammered in her ears. She took one step, then another. She picked up the group clearer now and determined they were arguing about what to do next.

Then, a floorboard creaked behind her.

She spun, but too late. A rough hand clamped down over her mouth, an arm hooked around her waist. Ingrid kicked and twisted, trying to scream, but the man was too strong, his grip iron-tight. He pulled her closer, and she struggled to breathe. He dragged her into a side room, slammed the door, and turned the flame of an oil lamp up.

"Well, what do we have here?" he said, grinning.

Ingrid recognized him immediately. The friend of the original man, the one she'd barely missed with her car when they escaped from the park.

"Spying, are we?" he asked.

Ingrid didn't answer. She tried to wrench free, but he shoved her into a chair and tied her wrists with a length of cord.

"Where's your friend?" he demanded.

"I don't know," Ingrid said.

The man lifted his arm and positioned himself to slap her,

but refrained.

"Where is your friend?" he asked again.

"I'm telling you, I have no clue."

The man slapped Ingrid across the right cheek, resounding like a rifle report. Her head snapped to the side, and she cried out in equal parts pain and frustration.

"Where's your friend?" he asked again.

Ingrid looked at him, tears welling in her eyes, her cheek flushing red.

He smirked. "It's okay. We'll find her."

He left, locking the door behind him.

Outside, Allie had heard the faint scuffle, a muffled thud, and a slammed door, and her stomach dropped. She looked through the two nearest windows and didn't see Ingrid anywhere. Panic flared, but she forced it down. It wasn't the first time a plan had gone sideways on her, and she was confident it wouldn't be the last. She just needed a moment to think.

She moved to the window and used her phone to capture what was happening. The men were getting restless. One of them stood, stretched, and produced a flask from his trench coat. After a long draw, he replaced it without offering anyone else a drink. The woman sat at the table, leaned back, and crossed her arms like she was trying to wait out a child's tantrum.

Allie saw Drake move ever so slightly. She could only imagine how uncomfortable and stiff he was since she didn't have any idea how long he'd been lying there.

Then she got it. The new plan arrived fast and dangerous. The woman and Asger wanted the treasure box more than anything. They'd followed the group all over Denmark trying to get it, and were willing to shoot them dead in a cave to retrieve it, so she guessed it had to have some significance to them. She could use that to her advantage.

Like a stealthy black cat, Allie moved back to the car. Grateful that Ingrid had left the keys in it for once, Allie popped the trunk. In it were Ingrid's pack containing the treasure box, the ax, and the dagger they'd taken from the tunnel. She needed more light than the trunk provided, so she activated the flashlight on her phone and set it at an angle that wouldn't show from outside the car.

Allie removed the ornate box from the pack and studied it carefully for the first time since they'd taken it. The lid depicted the four gods whose riddles they had solved earlier. In the center were Viking runes she couldn't read, so she snapped a photograph of it. She tried to remove the lid and found it wouldn't budge. Having gone through something similar earlier, she took the old coins from her pockets and placed one coin on each of the god's symbols and pressed them in with her thumb, each resulting in a click. Once all four were in place, the lid lifted away.

Allie opened the box. Inside she found a beautifully crafted Viking torque, and beside it, a scroll of parchment. Mindful of the curse, she carefully removed each object, placed them into Ingrid's backpack and set the pack gently in the backseat and covered it with her windbreaker. Next, she looked along the roadside, discovered three heavy rocks, placed them in the box, and closed it. From the top, she removed the coins, then picked up the box, grabbed her phone, and closed the trunk.

She tiptoed to the back of the house and entered through the creaking door. She held her breath as she waited, but no one came. Allie passed through the kitchen into the hallway. She saw lights ahead, assumed it was the living room, and pressed on, stopping in the shadows. From her perspective, she noticed the card table was in front of her, and four people sat there with their backs to her. Beyond them, she spotted Drake on the floor. He saw her, but his face remained as it was, displaying a steady, morose, and concerned look.

Allie listened for a moment.

"...we need to move tonight," the man in the trench coat

said. "Who cares about the Viking treasure? Don't we have enough?"

The woman stood and stepped toward the man. She held out an index finger and jabbed it into his chest as she spoke. "I say when we have enough. We will have the chest. I'm not sending the shipment until we get it."

"But the boat leaves at six," Asger said.

She turned around and stared at him. "I've already contacted the boat. They will leave when I tell them to, and not a second earlier."

"How are we going to get it?" Asger asked.

"Your friend has it, doesn't she? Call her and tell her to bring it or we'll kill him." Mette pointed at Drake. "If you need to, get him to convince her. Make a deal. She brings the box, and she gets her friend back. It's as easy as that."

Allie stepped back. She'd wondered briefly why they had held the conversation in English instead of Danish, and she realized it was for Drake's benefit. To let him know they were serious. She also realized they'd given too much of the plan away and Drake would never leave the farmhouse alive.

As she watched, Asger dug out his cell and made a call. From the room behind her, she heard a phone ring. Ingrid's phone.

Allie froze for a second and realized everyone saw her when they turned to see where the ringing was coming from. Rather than retreat, she stepped forward into the living room. She held up the treasure box for all to see.

Allie took another step and held the box higher. "You want this box? You have to make a deal. Let my friends go. Both of them. They leave; you get the box."

Mette produced her pistol and pointed it at Allie. "I can simply shoot you and take the box."

Allie shook her head. "There are three reasons you shouldn't. First, I've seen what's inside. I know it's delicate, and that it's probably worth a small fortune. If I drop the box, I'll probably destroy the contents. Second, there's a trick to getting this open. If you don't know the trick, you'll never see what's inside it. If you try to force your way in, you'll destroy what's inside. I understand the trick. You need me."

"And the third reason?" Mette asked, moving forward.

"You forgot about my other friend. She's with the police and on her way here. I'm live on the phone with them now, and they're listening to this call. You already have a kidnapping charge coming, do you really want to add three counts of murder?"

Asger sprang from his seat and grabbed Mette's arm. "She's right. Make the deal. We can be out of here in five minutes. I can't go to prison. I can't."

Mette turned to him. "You're such a gutless weasel. But in this case, you may be right. Go get the girl."

Allie stepped to one side as Asger moved toward her. She half-expected him to do something, but instead he walked right by. A minute later, he returned with Ingrid in tow.

"Get Drake out of here," Allie ordered.

Ingrid stopped and glanced from Allie to Asger to Mette.

"Go on," Mette said.

Ingrid moved to Drake and undid his bindings. Once free, she helped him get to his feet.

"Leave," Allie ordered.

Ingrid and Drake took tentative steps toward the front door, and once they realized no one would stop them, they quickly exited the house.

"Now, give me the box," Mette said.

Without answering, Allie moved to the front window and peered into the darkness. She breathed a sigh of relief when she saw Ingrid was taking Drake to the car and they weren't lying in wait hoping to rescue her. She waited until she saw Ingrid flash her flashlight twice, then stepped to the front door.

"Give me the box," Mette repeated, raising her gun again.

Allie swallowed. "Remember, if you shoot me, you lose your prize."

Mette lowered the gun and stepped back.

Allie nodded, and keeping the others in sight, set the box on the floor.

Asger stepped toward it as Allie put her hand in her pocket. "Wait. You'll need the key to get in."

"What key?" Asger asked.

"The coins. You've seen them, remember? The coins you told Geneva were worthless. Turns out they are quite the opposite."

Allie took her hand out of her pocket and took a step out the front door. She heard the honk of a car horn and knew it was time to leave.

"Here, catch," she said, throwing the coins into the room.

She turned and bolted. Ingrid had left the passenger door open for her, and Allie dove in, breathless. Tires spun on gravel as Ingrid threw the car into gear.

"You gave them the box?" Ingrid asked.

"Don't worry. The treasure is in the backseat, and they can't open it without the coins, anyway." Allie held one up. "I threw a bunch of kroner into the room, hopefully that will fool them."

"It didn't," Ingrid said, looking into the rearview.

Behind them, headlights from two cars flared.

"They're coming!" Allie shouted.

"I know," Ingrid replied. "Hold on!"

The chase tore down the dirt road, dust billowing in the moonlight. Although Ingrid tried to lose the pursuers, the headlights behind them stayed close, weaving through the turns.

"Go faster," Drake said from the backseat.

"I'm trying!" Ingrid said.

The road dipped sharply, cutting between dark fields and patches of woods. Allie twisted in her seat, watching as one car hit a rut and skidded sideways, slamming into a fence. The other car avoided the mess, stayed on their tail, and closed the gap.

"That's one down," Allie said.

"Not enough," Ingrid said through clenched teeth.

The remaining car, the one Asger drove, gained on them, headlights blinding in the mirror. A shot cracked in the night. The bullet pinged off the trunk. Ingrid swerved, almost lost control, and found the road again.

Another shot rang out, but missed them.

"Stream ahead!" Allie shouted suddenly. "There's a bridge out!"

Ingrid saw it too late. A small wooden bridge loomed ahead, but in front of it, blocking the road, was a sign announcing it was under construction. Ingrid slammed on the brakes, but the car skidded on the wet dirt, careening sideways. The front bumper destroyed the sign, the world tilted, and they plunged off the road into the shallow stream below.

Cold water exploded around them. For a moment, everything was noise and motion. A hiss erupted as the water hit the hot engine, and a groan of metal resounded when the car settled on the creek bed.

"Everyone okay?" Ingrid asked.

Allie coughed. "I think so. Drake?"

Drake was already trying to push the back door open. "I'm fine. We need to move before they get here."

Headlights cut through the dark again. Asger skidded to a stop on the road above, and a moment later he and Mette appeared above the car.

Allie's heart sank. "Oh, no."

Mette pointed her gun at Drake, who was the person closest to her. "Hand over the real coins now."

Allie and Ingrid exchanged a look.

Then, from the distance, a wail of sirens broke the quiet night.

Drake straightened. "It looks like you're out of time."

Mette and Asger looked at each other, then ran back toward

their car.

CHAPTER TWENTY

The full moon cast its light upon the countryside, partially illuminating the country lane, making it easier for Asger to determine where he was going. The Volkswagen hurtled along faster than its engine really wanted to go, and the random road ruts were tearing at the suspension. Asger's knuckles whitened on the steering wheel. An engine warning light blinked twice and faded out.

"Don't tell me to slow down," Asger said to his passenger through gritted teeth. "You'll only make me go faster."

Mette, sitting in the passenger seat with one hand braced against the dashboard, gave a short, humorless laugh. "I wouldn't dream of it, although the police behind us might appreciate your moderation."

"They'll appreciate nothing," he muttered, checking the rearview mirror. The blue lights still flickered half-a-mile back. They were too close for comfort, but too far for surrender. "There's no way I'm going to jail." Asger checked the mirror again. He counted at least five cars in pursuit, and he didn't dare to guess how many would be up ahead.

Asger punched the gas again. The car hit a dip in the dirt, flew airborne for a few feet, then slammed into the ground, its passengers bouncing in their seats.

"Watch it!" Mette yelled. "We can't risk breaking the box!" She leaned forward to check it and noticed the treasure miraculously hadn't moved from between her feet.

The sirens grew louder. Asger glanced at the rearview and realized the police had halved the distance.

Asger took the next bend sharply, tires squealing, and the Volkswagen skidded for an awful half-second before catching the road again. "Hold on," he said. "I might see a shortcut through the woods."

Mette didn't argue. Although she considered Asger to be far inferior to her in every way, she learned that his natural instincts were usually spot on. The car darted down a narrow track between trees, branches whipping against the windshield. Eventually, the forest swallowed the noise of the sirens.

Only when the sounds faded did Mette let herself breathe. "Do you think we've lost them?"

"For now," Asger said. "But we can't keep this up forever. And even if we did, we could only assume those goons you hired got captured already and will rat you out."

Mette chuckled.

"What?" Asger said.

"You mean rat you out. So far as they knew, you were the boss, and I was but your humble assistant."

"You didn't!" Asger stammered.

"I did. So, you better hope the police don't find you here, and I'd recommend a vacation. South America, perhaps?"

"Trust me," Asger growled. "If I go down, you're going with me."

Asger spotted a large willow tree and drove right toward it. He slowed, then pushed his way through the branches and parked the car next to the trunk. "This won't fool anyone forever, but if we're lucky, they'll pass right by us."

Asger and Mette exited the car. The air smelled of damp leaves and gasoline. Asger got to his knees and shined his flashlight under the car.

"Great. We've got a petrol leak," he said.

"Is this still drivable?" Mette asked.

"Probably. It's only a slow drip at this point, but I can't guarantee how far we will go."

"Fine. We'll drive it until we can't, then find another car," Mette said.

Mette retrieved the treasure box and placed it on the car's hood. She used her own cell to illuminate the box and marveled at the jewels attached to it. She ran her finger along each of the four circles, realizing they'd made a fool of her. Mette realized she couldn't break it open without destroying the contents, so she knew she needed to backtrack and get the real coins.

Asger leaned against the willow trunk, rubbing the back of his neck. "We could still turn ourselves in. Maybe if we explain…"

"Explain what?" Mette said. "That we were using our positions at the museum to smuggle artifacts out of the country? Or that we started out rescuing pieces from neglect and unwanted collections and ended up selling them to collectors who don't care where the objects came from? That we recovered items stolen during the war, then turned around and sold them?" She shook her head. "No. You understand as well as I do, they'll make examples of us, and we'll never see the outside of a prison again."

"Maybe we deserve that," Asger said.

Mette looked into his eyes. "Do you really believe that?"

He didn't answer.

It had begun innocently enough. They'd done their jobs, cataloging artifacts that came in from estate sales or treasure hunters, documenting the provenance of lost and forgotten art.

Then, a collector had offered Mette an obscene amount for a shipment of "unregistered" Roman coins. Then another for medieval jewelry with a forgotten paper trail. In Scandinavia, authentic Viking artifacts paid the most of all. Somewhere along the line, she brought Asger into the fold, and together, their ethics had slipped quietly out the back door.

Now the law had caught up with them.

"Where should we go?" Asger asked.

"I have an associate who lives about an hour from here. If we can get there, we'll be safe for a while."

The crackle of a radio interrupted her. Asger froze. The sound was faint but distinct. It was the static murmur of a police transmission, not far away.

"They're sweeping these woods," he whispered.

Mette grabbed the treasure box. "Come on. Let's get out of here."

Silently, they got into the car, and Asger started it up. He assumed once they left the tree cover, someone would spot them almost immediately. He shifted the car into gear and said a silent prayer.

Before they dared to move, headlights flooded the car interior, and they felt a jolt as a police car came bumper to bumper with them. Asger and Mette got jostled forward when another car hit them in the rear. They were trapped. Outside came the sounds of several car doors slamming, and voices shouting.

"I think we can still run for it," Mette said.

It was already too late. Before either of them did anything, the driver and passenger doors opened at once.

A voice barked. "Hands where we can see them!"

Asger raised his hands in surrender. Next to him, Mette pulled out her pistol. Rather than aiming at the police officer inches away, she pointed it under her chin. Before she had a chance to pull the trigger, the patrolman pulled it away and threw it into the grass. Beaten, Mette raised her hands.

As the handcuffs clicked into place, Mette looked at Asger. He met her gaze steadily and noticed she had a strange calm in her eyes.

"Don't say anything," Mette said to him. "Not yet. Not ever."

* * *

Back at the stream, Allie, Ingrid, and Drake were getting checked over by a police officer. When he determined none of the injuries were life-threatening, he handed them blankets. Rather than wait in the patrol car, they shared a spot on a pile of large wooden braces meant to repair the bridge.

Drake pointed into the stream. "You're never going to be able to rent another car as long as you live."

Ingrid shrugged. "That's fine. I can simply buy one when I need it, then sell it back."

"Or, perhaps you could take a cab. You shouldn't be driving," Drake teased.

Ingrid blew a raspberry at him, then took a drink of water from the bottle the police officer had been kind enough to give her.

"Whatever the treasure was, it probably got ruined," Ingrid bemoaned.

"I wouldn't say that," Drake said. "I rescued a few things from the car before I left the scene." He held up Ingrid's pack and then opened it. From it he took out an item wrapped in a soggy jacket.

"No, put that back," Ingrid said. "We'll look at it later when we're all alone."

Drake replaced the item and zipped up the bag. The trio watched in silence as the lights of an approaching patrol car got closer. After a few minutes, it stopped right in front of them. Out stepped the driver, Inspector Louise Jensen.

"We got them," the inspector said.

Ingrid nodded. "Good."

"And we found something of yours."

The passenger door opened, and Geneva approached with a wide smile on her face. "Hey gang! Did I miss out on anything?"

* * *

Two days later, the friends entered the National Museum of Denmark in Copenhagen. They approached the information desk, but didn't get a chance to speak when someone came up behind them.

"They're with me," Inspector Jensen said to the receptionist. "We have an appointment with the director."

The receptionist nodded and then made a quick phone call. After she hung up, she escorted the group to a conference room at the back of the museum. They each took a seat at the oval table, and the receptionist left. There, they waited for fifteen minutes before a man bounded into the room, excitement showing on his face.

"I'm Director Nielsen," he said as he walked around the table, getting names and shaking hands. He then took a chair, clasped his hands and leaned forward. "I understand you have something for us."

Ingrid nodded. She placed her pack on the table, opened it, and extracted the treasure box. Since she sat directly across from the director, she slid it across the table to him.

"My goodness, where did you find this?" he asked.

"That's a tale that will take a while to tell," Ingrid said. "Why don't you see what's inside?"

The director examined the box and noticed a series of runes. "Wise and brave, through riddles four, treasure's door you now restore. Riches are many, but wisdom is more. Take the gift, but heed the lore."

"Impressive," Allie said.

Nielsen's cheeks reddened with embarrassment. With his bright white hair and now red cheeks, he could have almost passed for Santa. "Thank you."

"You'll need these," Geneva said, passing the four coins to him.

He took the coins, along with instructions from Allie, and had the box open in short order.

"Oh, dear, Odin!" he exclaimed when he saw the treasure inside. He opened the scroll first. "You have proved worthy. Treasure is knowledge for those who seek. Carry it with honor. Let it guide your days with wisdom as Odin's eye guides the night." He set the scroll aside.

"Do you know what this is?" he said, donning a pair of gloves.

"A fancy necklace?" Drake asked.

"No. This is much more. You see, this is the Torque of the Gods! They forged this in an era when gods still walked the earth. It's said a smith created it based on a warrior's direction. The warrior bargained with the ravens of Odin for secrets of speech and command."

The director lifted the torque from the box and held it up for all to see. It was broad and heavy, fashioned from twisted strands of darkened gold and silver, wound together so tightly that they seemed to pulse with an inner current. As he moved, the twist pattern shifted in the light, as though the metal itself was breathing.

Each end ended in a raven's head. One wrought from obsidian-black silver, the other from a pale, almost white, gold. Tiny garnets, dark as drying blood, made up the raven's eyes. The eyes glimmered faintly every time they caught a ray of light.

Along the inner curve, where the torque rested against the throat, the smith had etched runes as fine as a cat's hair.

"These runes spell out the fragments of an ancient charm. The thrall shall bow to the word, the king shall bow to the will," the director said.

"What's that mean?" Ingrid asked.

"There's a whole legend behind this," the director said as he carefully returned the torque to the box. "It's said to have been forged for a warrior-poet who wanted dominion not through battle, but through persuasion. Legends claim he journeyed to the roots of Yggdrasil, which was a sacred tree. There, he found one of Odin's ravens, Muninn, tangled in the branches of time. He freed the bird, and in gratitude, it whispered the runes of mastery over men into his ear. The warrior carried those secrets back and bound them to this torque. When he wore it, his mere words could quell rebellions, charm kings, and turn foes into allies. Entire armies would kneel before him, convinced they did so of their own will. When he tried to command the sea itself, the sea swallowed him whole, and the torque disappeared into legend."

"What about the curse? Where it engulfs the wearer in a column of fire?" Ingrid asked.

The director looked at her and smiled. "It doesn't do that. At least no story has ever said it does. Although there is a curse of sorts. Even though it grants the wearer's command, it hungers for obedience and slowly bends its bearer toward arrogance and isolation. Over time, those who wear it too long lose their own voice to the one the torque gives them."

Ingrid sat back in her chair. "That's fascinating."

"What's going to happen to it now?" Allie asked.

"Now this torque, along with the treasure box and coins, will go on display in this museum. You've restored a magnificent piece of Viking history, of Denmark's history, to us, and we're grateful."

"One last question," Drake said, raising a finger in the air. "We understand that during the war, Hitler himself was searching for this thing. Had he found it, would things have turned out differently?"

Director Nielsen stared at Drake, pondering the possibilities. "Thankfully, that's a question we'll never need the answer to."

* * *

The next day, Ingrid decided to visit Asger, so she journeyed to the Copenhagen Prison. The prison was one of those cheerless modern buildings with clean lines, pale walls, and a faint smell of disinfectant. A guard led her down a corridor to a small visiting room, where Asger waited behind a table.

He looked older than she remembered. His hair, usually neatly combed, had a disheveled look to it, like he'd awoken from a nap in order to meet with her. He carried a look of tiredness in his eyes that no amount of sleep could fix.

"I didn't think you'd come," he said.

"I almost didn't," Ingrid admitted. "But I needed to hear it from you."

He smiled faintly. "You always preferred facts over rumors."

They sat in silence for a moment. The hum of fluorescent lights filled the space.

"Why, Asger?" she asked. "You had a good life. A great job, friends who trusted you. Why throw it all away?"

He looked down at his hands. "It wasn't supposed to be like this. When we started, Mette and I thought we were preserving history. You know, saving it from dust and neglect. Then we realized how many people would pay to own a piece of the past, and once you put a price on it, it stops being history and starts becoming temptation." He glanced at her. "You should know that better than anyone. I've read about your exploits in the articles, the treasures you and your friends have found."

"Everything we've found we donated to museums and other

places. And I understand the curiosity, but not the betrayal. We were friends for a long time, Asger."

"You remember those Viking legends we used to read about as kids, don't you? Fantastical treasures that could give the owner ultimate power?" he said.

"I remember."

He leaned forward slightly. "When you and your friend showed up in my office, I realized you'd found a real clue. A trail. I told Mette it was probably just a legend, but she believed, and the more I followed you, the more I believed, too. She thought if we could find it, we could make the score of a lifetime. We'd have enough money to walk away from everything. Disappear. Start over."

"And you went along with it."

"Yes. Like I said, the closer you got, the more I believed."

"You were looking for the ultimate power, just to sell it off to the highest bidder?" Ingrid asked.

He nodded.

"It was there," Ingrid admitted. "In that treasure box we found in the caves."

He looked up sharply. "It was really there? It really exists?"

"Yes."

"What was it?" Asger leaned forward, hungry for an answer.

"You'll need to visit the National Museum to find out. If you ever get out of here, that is. One last question. How did you always know where we were?"

Asger gave a sly smile. "That day you came to see me. I knew exactly what you had, and I knew I needed to keep an eye on you. When I saw you out, I slipped a tracker into your backpack."

Ingrid nodded, resisting the urge to check her clothing right then and there.

They sat in silence again; the words hanging between them like dust motes in sunlight.

Asger closed his eyes. "I'm sorry for everything I've done.

I've ruined my life."

Ingrid stood to leave. "And some friendships."

Asger looked up at her, guilt and gratitude mingling in his expression. "Tell your friends I'm sorry," he mumbled. "For everything."

"I will," she said, though she wasn't sure it was true.

As Ingrid walked out, the guard holding the door for her, she couldn't help but think of the Torque of the Gods laying in the museum's vault, pulsing faintly, waiting for its next bearer.

Outside, the afternoon light was soft and golden again, just as it had been during every day of their trip. The world, it seemed, had a way of circling back on itself with old secrets, old friends, old regrets.

"Are you ready to go?" Geneva asked as Ingrid approached their new rental car.

"I am," Ingrid said.

Geneva leaned in and gave her best friend a hug.

"Come on, you two, there's a cache just around the corner," Drake said, holding up his phone for all to see.

"Lead on, my man," Geneva said.

Drake led the group around the block and across the street to the parking lot of a pharmacy.

"Think it's an LPC?" Drake asked, following the arrow on his phone.

"It would surprise me if it weren't a light pole cache," Allie said. "Parking lots always seem to have them."

Drake went to the light pole nearest to his coordinates and lifted the metal skirt with a screech, revealing a small plastic container underneath. While Drake held the skirt, Geneva grabbed the container and opened it up. Inside she found the log and passed it around for her friends to sign. As she waited, she examined the contents of the container.

"Hey! Guess what I found!" Geneva said with a lilt of joy in her voice.

"Oh no," Drake said. "Not another ancient coin."

"Nope," Geneva said, holding up a metal tag. "It's a trackable!"

"Fun!" Allie said as she placed the paper log back in the box. "What's the number?"

Geneva studied the tag for a moment, turning it so she could see the numbers in the sunlight. "It's N6FG4Q."

"Sweet," Drake said, "It's always fun to find a trackable We'll have to remember to log it."

"You know what else is fun to find?" Allie asked.

"What?" Drake asked.

Allie grinned. "Ice cream. Come on, let's get some ice cream, then we can continue our adventures."

ABOUT THE AUTHOR

Dan DeKoning was born and raised in Milwaukee, Wisconsin, and currently lives in Northwest Arkansas with a very loving cat.

He is a storyteller and poet who loves to write in a variety of genres and themes. He is also a voracious reader who loves to read anything he can get his hands on.

When he's not writing, you can find him hunting for treasures in used bookstores, or out exploring the planet, or geocaching, or searching for adventures and stories to tell.

BIBLIOGRAPHY

Fiction
Déjà Vu
The Haunting of Hyacinth House
How Deep the Darkness
Baker's Crossing
How Bright the Light

Geocaching Mystery Series
The Cacheland Conspiracy
The Quincy Bay Quandary
The Secret of the Seven Valleys
The Geocaching Mystery Omnibus – Volume 1
Search for the Serpent's Stone
Deception in Denmark

Codi Cassidy Cozy Mystery Series
Acoustics and Alibis
Ballads and Bloodshed
Codas and Calibers
Codi Cassidy Omnibus – Volume 1

Poetry Collections
Lost and Found
Random Thoughts

Nonfiction
The Geocaching County Tracker